BLOOD BETRAYED

SONS OF NAVARUS
BOOK 2

K.M. SCOTT

WRITING AS
GABRIELLE BISSET

BLOOD BETRAYED

I am everything forbidden. I am vampire.

Haunted by betrayal, Saint hides in the human world,
giving his heart to no one and finding the only solace
from his past in the arms of human women. Now as the
Archons begin their takeover of the vampire world, this
Son of Navarus has been marked for death.

Summoned to defeat the Archons by the world that
shunned him, Saint must face his past and Solenne, the
woman he loved and lost a century ago, for only in
accepting her will his body and soul finally find salvation.

Blood Betrayed is a work of fiction. Names, characters, places, and events are the products of the author's imagination. Any resemblance to events, locations, or persons, living or dead, is coincidental.

2013 Copper Key Media LLC

Published in the United States

ISBN: 978-1-955335-36-2

For every woman who ever questioned if her memory stayed with someone long after she was gone, Saint is the answer.

1

I am everything forbidden.
I am a haunted creature.
I am darkness and shadow.
I am vampire.

Real betrayal — the kind that tears the heart and soul out – is never a solo endeavor. True betrayal needs another villain to share the guilt. Together, two can harm so much more than one.

Declan Collins stood silently, his eyes focused on the far walls of the Archon's chambers. On and on the men and women around him continued to debate the case against him. Their words enveloped him, a jumbled mess that threatened to smother him.

What the fuck did he care what they thought? They only knew what they'd been told. Nothing more. Nothing real.

He'd given up his chance to defend himself, against the advice of his lawyer who'd begged him to help — to do anything — to help his case. What was the use? Nothing they could do to him could be any worse than what he could do to himself. Whatever the verdict, it would pale in comparison to the torture he'd already begun inflicting on himself.

It mattered little that he wasn't responsible. When did that ever truly matter? What mattered was that he'd been who he'd been accused of being, just not how they said. Defending himself would've only meant hurting someone he loved, and the end result would have been the same.

Maybe he was guilty of this crime, but he wasn't cruel. No matter how much cruelty he'd endured and would live with the rest of his time on Earth.

"Declan Collins."

The Archon's hollow voice roused him from his thoughts, and he trained his eyes on the man who sat behind an enormous old desk. Lawyers and other officials fell silent, and Declan felt his own lawyer gently touch him on the shoulder, as if to offer condolences on the verdict they both knew was coming.

"You stand charged with breaking one of the most sacred laws of our kind. The relationship between sire and vampire is one of the cornerstones of our world, and you are accused of dishonoring this relationship. Before I pronounce my verdict, do you have anything to say in your defense?"

Declan felt their gaze on him as everyone in the room waited to hear even a word that would show he wasn't the monster he appeared to be. If he wanted to, he could speak words to disprove everything that had been said about him.

Love.

Devotion.

Betrayal.

He said nothing and waited to hear his punishment.

"As you refuse to defend yourself, I have to assume the

charges are indeed true and sentence you to a solitary life with your own vampires for a term of no less than ten years."

At the heavy sound of the Archon's gavel, everyone in the room resumed their activity. His lawyer spoke of the leniency of the Archon and his good fortune to only be shunned from the rest of the vampire world for ten years, but Declan ignored him.

A solitary life with only vampires of his own. He had none. No soul on earth had made him wish to bring them into the world he was now forced to leave.

Ten years, one hundred years. What did it matter? No amount of time would change what had happened. The Archon had done him a favor. He didn't belong in this world. He belonged in the world he'd been forced to leave the night his sire had robbed death of its due.

AN ICY WIND bit at him, but even the feel of it whipping against his skin couldn't dull the pain of hunger that tore at his insides. How long it had been since he'd tasted the blood of one of his own he couldn't remember. To do so always reminded him of her...

The streets he strode down one after another remained deserted, denying him of even that brief respite from his pain that human blood provided. Did no one live in this godforsaken village full of empty streets? If only he could find one, maybe two souls to give him what he needed.

Snowflakes flew into his face, sticking to his eyelashes and blinding him momentarily, and he was forced to halt his march down a darkened alley. Through the whiteout, he felt his way over the face of the building next to him, running his hands over the weather–worn bricks to a doorway. Still blinded by the storm, he slid his hands down the wooden door to the doorknob and turned it sharply to the right as he pushed all his weight against the entrance.

Inside the darkened house, his eyes quickly adjusted to the blackness surrounding him. Was this place abandoned like the rest of Suceava seemed to be? Slowly, he scanned the room hoping to sense a warm body nearby but found nothing.

Saint inhaled deeply and his nose located what his eyes hadn't. Someone — at least one person — was in the building with him. Silently, he moved toward the door and began ascending the staircase. The scent of the human grew stronger with each step, and as he reached the top stair, he heard the faintest sound of someone breathing.

Searching the room in front of him, he saw a figure crouched in the corner clutching something. Three steps closer and he saw the human he'd sensed one floor below. In the darkness, a woman held a baby tightly to her chest as she looked up at Saint with eyes wide with fear.

"Please...please don't hurt us," she begged in a shaky voice.

He extended his hand and in the darkness touched hers. It trembled against his palm. Closing his fingers around it, he gently pulled her to her feet. "Come."

Saint touched the baby's head, tenderly running his fingertips over the soft down before he whispered, "Lay the child down."

The woman obeyed his command without question

and silently placed the baby in his crib. She turned with hesitation from him after whispering a promise to keep them safe from harm and stared up at Saint.

Her expression showed her fear, and he gently ran the back of his hand down her cheek to calm her. "I won't hurt the child if you give me what I need."

In a tiny voice, she replied, "I have nothing but him, but take whatever you may find in this house. Please just spare my life and my son's."

Saint studied her in the darkness, noting her eyes so full of fear of him were also beautiful and expressive. Her long hair was dark and fell back from her face as she looked up at him. "I don't want your life. Just your blood," he whispered as he trailed his fingers along the tendrils that hung over her shoulders. "Give me what I need, and you and he will remain unharmed."

He heard the sharp intake of her breath as he explained what he'd take from her. "I promise you won't be hurt."

"Vampire?" she asked softly.

"Vampire."

As if resigned to her fate, the woman moved to the bed near the child's crib and sat down as Saint followed. Seated next to her, he began to speak the hypnotic chant into her ear and felt her body calm next to his.

"Tell me your name."

"Alina."

Taking her face in his hands, he turned her head to look at him. "Alina, I take from you because I must. You'll feel no pain."

He watched her close her eyes in silent permission, and with his hands still cradling her face, he bent his head to her neck. The first brush of her warm skin against his lips brought his fangs into position. Inhaling deeply, he smelled the gentle scent of her skin, exciting him.

Blood wasn't all he hungered for. The thought of taking so much more from her made his cock harden, and his fangs cut into his lower lip in need. Stubbornly, he forced himself to remember he should only have her blood.

Pressing into the tender skin of her neck, he had to wait only for that long moment before the human body gave up what he craved. She cried out just once, a soft keening sound, and then fell silent as he began to pull gently at her vein.

Her blood tasted sweet and tangy on his tongue, and he savored it as it slid toward his throat. Never as potent or fulfilling as the blood of one of his vampires, or any vampire for that matter, human blood could take the edge off the constant hunger that had been with him for longer than he could remember.

With each pull he felt the hunger recede into the darkness inside him. Alina's hand moved to cradle his neck, and the soft caress of her fingers on his closely shaved head made the urge to take more than blood surge in him.

Moaning against her skin, he reveled in her touch as she gently stroked the back of his head. The need for the closeness of another grew to match the earlier need for blood and lifting his head from her neck, he saw a look of desire on her beautiful face.

"Please tell me your name," she begged.

Knowing he would dissolve her memory as he left, he answered, "Declan."

"Declan," she repeated in a dreamy voice, as if his name pleased her.

He ran the pad of his thumb across her bottom lip and imagined sucking on its full plumpness. At the corner of her mouth, he rubbed his finger over her soft skin, touching the faintest hint of a frown. She turned her head and took his thumb into her mouth. Softly at first, she sucked just the tip, making his mind dance at the thought of her mouth on his cock. Desire for more pressed into him, overwhelming his strength to fight it.

Nearby the soft coo of the baby as he began to rouse from sleep made Alina turn her attention to the crib, leaving Saint to watch as her desire turned to concern.

"I am all he has in this world," she said quietly looking down into the crib.

Sadness pinched at his heart as he listened to her words. Whatever the world had seen fit to deal her, she had that one soul to love and who loved her in return. And him? He had everything a man could wish for and more. A vampire for one hundred years, he was eternally young, free to do as he pleased when he pleased, a servant to no other soul on earth. But still she had more than he.

As self-pity threatened to choke him, he did as he'd always done and gave into the only thing that had ever been able to make him forget all that he so desperately tried not to remember.

Greed.

It had given him the strength to get up each night, the power to amass the wealth and possessions that meant a life of luxury full of whichever vice he preferred to deliver the contentment he craved. Encircling her arm with his hand, he pulled her to him and held her close. Brown eyes looked up in surprise at him, but the demon inside saw nothing but what it desired.

"Come. He'll be fine."

Through a door they entered a smaller room, empty except for a singular armoire on the far wall. Need reared up in him and he roughly pushed her back against the sturdy piece of furniture. Whatever affect his hypnotic words had produced earlier remained just enough for her to still want what he wanted, and she put up no struggle as he quickly stripped the clothes from her body.

Almost a century of experience took over, and Saint's mind went blank as he performed the motions that would give him what he wanted. She'd enjoy it, as all the others had, but he'd feel nothing inside. Never had another's actions been so rote yet so pleasurable.

His hands cupped her full breasts as he dipped his head to capture a soft nipple in his mouth. Flicking the tip of his tongue over it, he brought it to a hardened peak and softly bit down, eliciting a sweet moan from Alina. Pulling him closer, she pressed her hands against the back of his head, signaling her desire for him to continue. Her passionate mews spurred him on, and he dropped to his knees to taste her moist sex.

Hidden within her soft curls was the tiny spot that he sought out with his tongue. With his thumbs, he gently opened her up to gaze upon her gorgeous pink cunt. Softly, he flicked his tongue over her exposed clit, loving the sound of her needy moans each time he stroked the tender knot of nerves that quivered under his touch.

This vice — making love to human women — was one of his favorites, and he sought it out as often as life allowed. Unlike other vampires, he didn't have sex with those he sired or any other vampires. For almost a century, he'd only been with human women.

What should have been physically pleasurable was more a means to an emotional end. No doubt he enjoyed being inside a woman, as he would with Alina in a few minutes, his cock pressing against the soft walls of her cunt. But the end was the goal. In those brief moments as a woman's body closed around him signaling her climax, he wasn't alone.

Then it would end and he'd leave, knowing for at least a short time he'd made another soul happy and stolen some of that happiness for himself.

Saint rose to his full height and licked his lips to enjoy the taste of Alina. Excited to feel what he'd temporarily denied her, she tore at his clothes as she clawed at the fabric to feel his skin under her fingers. Aroused by her eagerness, he shrugged out of his clothes with little effort, pleased by the surprised look of happiness that came across her face.

"Little trick we vampires can do," he teased as he lifted her and moved to wrap her legs around him.

"Can you do anything else?" she asked shyly as she laced her fingers at the back of his neck and stared into his eyes.

Nodding, he placed his hands on the small of her back and pulled her toward his stiff cock. Slowly, he pressed into her warm and willing body, and when he was buried inside her, their bodies pressing against one another, he whispered, "Take from me, Alina. Take from me as I take from you."

With the first thrust of his cock, she pressed her lips against his, devouring him with her passion. He had no idea of what her life entailed other than the child in the next room and the sensations she was creating in him each time she tipped her hips upward to take him as deeply as her body could, and he didn't care. He'd give her the pleasure that would relieve a few moments of his loneliness, and she'd give him the blood he needed. No one would be hurt, and when he left, he wouldn't even be a memory in her mind.

As he thought this, he pumped into her cunt and focused only on that moment of sublime bliss she'd give him as she came. Each thrust shook the heavy wooden cabinet and Alina clung to him as he inched her body closer to climax. Her soft panting filled his ears, intermingled with moans and desperate pleas for him to continue.

He wouldn't stop. He needed that feeling too much.

His mouth moved to her neck for one last taste of her blood. No longer hungry, he sunk his fangs into her skin knowing it never failed to bring a woman to the edge he'd eagerly enjoy taking Alina over. Each draw on her vein made her beg for more and made his anticipation grow.

She raked her nails down his back as the first hint of her release was born, making him pump into her faster as he yearned for that moment as much or even more than she when her body would surrender completely to his.

"Declan..." she cried softly into the darkness of the room. "I... please don't stop."

As the beginning of her orgasm took hold of her, he left her neck and braced his hands on the cabinet behind her. Her body contracted around his cock and she came, and what he wanted she finally gave him.

Closing his eyes, he felt the blissful feeling of pure pleasure wash over him. Alina's body spasmed its ecstasy and he felt his own climax begin on top of hers, flooding her insides.

And then the world stopped around them. Alina became the only soul that existed for him in those incredible moments when he knew, beyond any doubt, that he'd brought her happiness. In that happiness, he found the closeness of another he'd searched for each night for almost one hundred years.

Then it was gone.

Saint returned to Alina's neck and closed the holes he'd made when he fed from her. When he raised his head, she kissed him tenderly on the lips, but the magic that had touched them in their joining was lost.

Gently, he moved out of her and set her on her feet on the floor. Cupping her face in his hands, he looked down into the sweetness that gazed up at him. The effects of the hypnosis would vanish when he spoke the words, but before that he wanted to take one last look at her.

"Alina, thank you for what you've given me."

Without another word, he led her to the bed next to her son and lifted her in his arms. Placing her down, he lay next to her and in the darkness chanted the ancient words to make her forget.

IN THE LAST hour before dawn, Saint walked the path he'd taken from Vasilije's home in the old monastery just outside of town. The storm had ended, leaving a layer of fresh snow, and he braced against the bitter cold that crept into his bones. Each step away from Alina was another step back toward the loneliness of every waking moment of his life. But this was his fate.

Crossing the field that separated the monastery from the town, he sensed the night began to lose its hold and hurried to reach Vasilije's before the sun gained the world. As he entered the house, he was met by the tense stares of the rest of the Sons of Navarus who were assembled just inside the door, each focused intently on him.

Vasilije stepped forward with a look of inquisition on his face. "Where have you been?"

"It's been a long time since I was young enough to have a curfew, dad. Where I've been is my own fucking business. Now if you don't mind, the sun's about to come up and I'd like to go to my room in your vampire Holiday Inn."

As he attempted to move past Vasilije, Dante taunted him. "Have a nice night out, Saint? Find any poor peasant girls to take the edge off?"

Before he could tell Dante exactly how to fuck himself, Saint felt Vasilije's hand on his arm. Looking down at where his hand lay, he said, "I suggest you remove your fucking hand and let me pass, Vasilije."

"Little touchy tonight, Saint? No luck with the local girls?" Dante goaded.

"Enough, Dante! We don't have time for this," Vasilije barked. Turning to face Saint, he continued, "You need to come with us."

"Why? It's almost dawn. Whatever we need to talk about we can do later. I'm not in the mood to talk any more shop today."

Yanking his arm from Vasilije's hold, Saint stepped forward, but his progress was halted by Ramiel, the only son big enough physically stop him. "Something's happened, Saint. We need to act."

Saint looked from one man to the next and saw each had the same look of concern on his face. What could have happened? He'd already lost his only brother because of the Archons, and he had no other family.

"They've taken everything they could. There's nothing left."

"Saint," Vasilije began. "It's you."

Instantly, Saint knew what he'd say next.

"You're the one they're after now."

2

Vasilije led the way to the meeting room and settled in behind the antique oak desk as the rest of the Sons took their places around the room. Another guest would join them in a few minutes, but before that, they had to convince Saint to do something he'd rarely done in the years Vasilije had known him.

Obey.

"So what are you saying? They still want you and we're not having long-faced meetings about that."

Saint's surly attitude wasn't a good sign. He wasn't going to fall in line easily.

"That's different."

"How?"

Vasilije sat back in his chair and folded his arms. "They don't know about this place. And there's Sasa."

Saint raised his eyebrows. "Oh, I get it. Because you're not single..." He suddenly stopped his train of thought and shook his head. "No, I don't get it. And what the hell do you mean they don't know about this place?"

"You're going to have to go into hiding. We can't risk the Archons finding you here. Ramiel and Thane are too important, and we can't move them."

"Explain to me why you don't have to go into hiding. Don't you put them in danger by staying here too?"

Vasilije remained silent for a long moment before asking Sion to close the door. Lowering his voice, he explained, "I don't want Sasa to hear this. They think I'm dead already. One of my vampires gave his life to complete the illusion. So I don't put anyone in danger."

Saint mumbled something and then asked, "Where are you asking me to go?"

The sharpness of his tone when he said "asking" didn't go unnoticed. Saint had been quite clear in his disgust for the idea that any one of them, especially Vasilije, was the leader able to order him around. It didn't help that the two of them hadn't liked one another since the night Vasilije had turned Teagan. And then after a problem between the brothers, Saint had cut himself off from everyone associated with Teagan.

Walking around the desk, Vasilije faced Saint. "We believe we've located a place for you to stay for a while until we can get more of your vampires' help."

Nico stepped out from near a bookcase and stood beside Vasilije. "We need you safe to fight the Archons, but your vampires have been slow to..." Hesitating as if to find the right words, he looked at Vasilije and finally said, "Slow to come around."

Saint smiled fakely, nodding his head. "I know what you're thinking, and I don't fucking care. Just because I don't rule over mine like a dictator doesn't mean they're any less devoted. Just tell me where this place is."

Before Vasilije could answer, the door opened and in walked Sasa with another woman. They'd barely closed the door behind them when Saint's thin veneer of civility evaporated in front of everyone's eyes.

"What is this?" he asked angrily. Turning back from glaring at the strawberry-blonde next to Sasa, he faced Vasilije with a look of pure rage. "What the fuck is this?"

"Sorry I'm late, Vasilije," the woman said. "I hope I didn't interrupt anything."

"No, we were just discussing..."

Saint cut him off in mid-sentence. "No, we weren't. I'm done with this."

As he spun around to leave, Vasilije grabbed him by the arm and pulled him back. "Saint, hold on." Seeing that he had his attention, at least for the moment, Vasilije nodded toward the door to signal the rest of the Sons to leave.

Once they and Sasa had left, he relaxed against the edge of the desk and dropped Saint's arm. "Let's talk. We all know each other. How long has it been since you and Solenne saw one another?"

Solenne touched Saint's sleeve and smiled warmly at him. "It's been a long time. How have you been?"

Ignoring her, Saint pulled his arm away. "What the fuck is this, Vasilije? Why is she here?"

"She's going to help you hide out for a while."

"No."

Vasilije folded his arms across his chest. "She's perfect for the job. She's helping us spy on the Archons and she has her house in France that's secluded enough that no one can find you."

"No."

"Vasilije, would it be better if I go?" Solenne asked.

"Yes," Saint answered in a nasty tone.

"Solenne, give us a minute." Vasilije said as he escorted her to the door.

Alone, the two men stood silently until Saint spoke and Vasilije heard the anguish in his voice. "Not her."

"Saint, she's the best chance we have until more of your vampires come forward to help. As one of Teagan's vampires, she wants to do anything she can to keep us safe and get back at the Archons who killed her sire."

"Anyone else. Just not her."

"Plus, she's agreed to give you blood while you're at her house."

Saint backed up, shaking his head. "No. I don't drink from any vampires but my own."

"We don't have that option yet, Saint."

"This is what I get for not being an overbearing fuck like you," Saint mumbled as he turned his face away.

"I don't see what the problem is. Solenne and you go way back, and she's one of Teagan's. Plus she's easy to look at. Christ, you'd think we'd set you up with someone who looked like a warden at some women's prison."

"How long?" Saint asked, his shoulders hunched in resignation.

"Just until we can know you've got some of your vampires behind you."

Saint scowled and sat down heavily in a nearby chair. The look on his face seemed odd to Vasilije considering he was about to be holed up in a French country house with a woman willing to risk her life to help him.

Saint's preference for human women was well-known, but Vasilije couldn't believe he'd see his time in

France with Solenne as a chore. He was cantankerous and difficult on his best days, for certain, but he wasn't crazy. Surely, even he could see the benefits this arrangement could offer.

Vasilije called Solenne back into the room and after bringing her up to speed with Saint's agreement, albeit reluctant, to the plan, he moved on to more important matters. "What else have you found other than Saint being the new target?"

"Not much yet," she said shaking her head. "They just found out about you and there's been a lot of celebrating. Lots of patting one another on the back for getting you."

"Nice," Vasilije said, disgusted by the actions of his own kind. "One of their own dies, and it's time for champagne. At least we know Brandon's ruse worked. I can't thank him enough. None of us can."

Brandon. The thought of his taking the stake for him touched Vasilije more than he could express. The last time he'd seen him before leaving for New Orleans, he'd been the picture of a lost soul, the happiness gone from him as if it had been drained out of his very soul when Arden had succumbed to a hunter's stake eight months earlier. That he'd sacrifice his own life for Vasilije and what the Sons were trying to do without being asked showed the depth of his pain.

He only hoped he'd have the courage to do the same if he lost Sasa.

"I'm sorry for your loss, Vasilije. I know how it feels to lose one you care for."

Solenne lowered her head and sighed. He understood her pain at the loss of her sire. He'd felt it all those years ago when Nina had been staked right before his eyes.

Still felt it in quiet moments when his mind drifted back to her.

"I know, Solenne. I miss him too."

Nodding in silence, she forced a smile and then looked over to Saint, who sat grimacing at the two of them. "I'm sorry about Teagan."

Slowly, he rose from his chair and walked to stand in front of her. A look of hatred settled into his features and when he spoke, his words came out as if they were hissed.

"I hadn't seen my brother for almost one hundred years because of you. Don't give me your sympathy. I don't want it."

Vasilije watched as Saint's expression hardened even more. Solenne stared back in sadness, obviously hurt by his words. "I think it's time you two got on your way. Solenne, keep us up to date with what's happening with the Archons. And be safe. If they find out what you're up to, pet, they won't hesitate to stake you too."

"I will. And don't worry about this. I won't let you down."

"Just let me know as soon as I'm done doing my time," Saint said in disgust as he left.

LOOKING around the eighteenth-century French country house, Saint saw that little had changed since the last time he'd been there. Expensively furnished, Solenne's home had been some important sire's until she'd decided that the French countryside offered little of the excitement an ancient vampire craved. At least that was the story Solenne had told. Who knew if it were true.

As he stared up at the crystal chandelier above his head, he said what he wished would be the last words he'd have to say to her. "Just tell me where my room is and where I can work out."

Solenne stood staring at him, and he felt her eyes boring holes through him.

"Saint, I'd hoped we could put the past behind us to work together. Can we at least talk?"

He lowered his gaze to meet hers and saw ocean blue eyes wide with hope staring back at him. That she could think that giving him some doe-eyed look and meaningless words would be enough to erase everything that had happened only made him more enraged about the situation.

"I'm not interested in talking or taking some stroll down memory lane. Just point me to my room and where I can work out."

The fiery look that instantly filled her eyes showed she was the same Solenne from all those years ago. He knew that oh-so-helpful woman from Vasilije's was just an act.

"It doesn't have to be like this. I'd hoped you'd be a bigger man and see how we could work together. I see you're the same man you've always been, unfortunately."

The same man he'd always been? As if he'd been to blame for any past problems between them. Fucking Vasilije and his plans! Squinting his eyes, he pushed down his anger and explained just how this arrangement was going to work.

"Solenne, here's how we're playing this. Once you tell me where I can sleep and where I can work out, we won't have to see each other much, assuming there's food in this house."

Saint stared down at her feeling pleased about laying down the law. Vasilije may have given her the impression that this was going to be her show, but she had another thing coming if she thought that was reality.

"Saint, we'll have to see each other so you can feed from me. I told Vasilije I'd be willing to..."

"No. And if you want me to stay here, I'm either going to go out each night or you're going to have to find me human females to feed from."

The effect of his words was immediate, and the stunned expression on her face pleased him more than it should have.

"Humans? Why would you choose to feed from humans when you can have my blood?"

The sound of hurt in her voice was unmistakable, and somewhere deep inside Saint loved it. Now to finish what he'd started. "You know why they call me Saint, don't you, Solenne?"

The hurt in her tone moved to her eyes and with a catch in her voice, she said, "You don't expect me to be your pimp, do you? I won't do it."

"Then I'll be leaving each night to find blood. Or maybe I won't be staying at all."

Saint headed toward the front door, but Solenne caught up with him just as his hand landed on the doorknob. Turning back to look at her, he saw he'd won this first match between them.

"I'm only doing this because you're important to the other Sons. I don't give a damn who you sleep with, but remember this is my house."

"Well, since you'll be choosing the women, I'm sure we won't have any problems."

Solenne regained her composure and matter-of-factly pointed him in the direction of his bedroom and the exercise room before she turned on her heels. As she walked away, the anger at his words came out in each pounding step she took.

"Solenne?"

Saint intentionally took the edge off his voice when he said her name, sure she'd refuse to listen if he didn't. She stopped her furious march and slowly turned to face him, her eyes once again full of hope.

"Yes, Saint?" she said in that sweet voice she'd used with Vasilije.

"Anything but redheads. And have someone here tonight when I wake up. Make sure she's willing. I don't want to fight for blood when I first get up."

Solenne's face grew flushed with anger, and for a moment, Saint swore she would lunge at him. Instead, she ran her hands through her strawberry-blonde hair and plastered a stiff smile on her face before storming out.

Nice to see you again, sweetheart.

THE BEDROOM he'd stay in during what was quickly feeling like his incarceration was as nice as the rest of the house. A king-sized antique bed faced a fireplace, and he had his own bathroom.

Not bad for a prison.

"Maybe I won't have to see her except when she brings me French farm girls," he said with a grin as he laid back to relax on the bed. He didn't have much experience with French women—farm or otherwise—but he suspected they'd be much like any other human female. In all his travels around the world, he hadn't found much difference among human women.

Not that he necessarily paid attention. His time with them was a means to an end. More truthfully, two ends. He needed blood as a vampire to keep him connected to his world, and since none of his vampires were nearby, he'd drink from a human. And he needed that release sex provided—that moment of bliss that quieted the demons and memories.

That he only slept with human females had earned him the nickname "Saint" and a status as some kind of oddity in the vampire world. The sexual joining of sire and vampire was considered to be the most sublime facet of being a vampire sire, and that first taste of a newly-turned vampire's blood slowly teasing her sire's tongue as he entered her was a moment of sheer ecstasy.

Or so he'd heard.

Never with any of the hundreds of females he'd sired had Saint slept with one of his vampires. Their turning had always been the same as with the males he'd sired. Of course, when his female vampires heard about what they'd missed out on from others, they asked and even begged for that closeness with him, only to be denied again and again.

The last vampire he'd made love to would be the only vampire to share that with him. He'd gone nearly one hundred years since then. He'd go another hundred or as long as he walked the Earth only sleeping with human women. That was part of his penance. He'd done it for so long, it was part of who he was.

In his limbs, he felt the sun begin to rise higher above the horizon, but restlessness kept him from some much-needed sleep. Being back in this house brought memories of Teagan back once again.

How many nights since hearing of his death had he spent thinking of him? Thoughts of a lifetime ago and the closeness of two brothers made vampire on the same night but by two very different sires crept into his mind.

His brother's sire, the son-of-a-bitch who'd consigned him to this place so full of the past, was nothing like his own sire. Where Vasilije was overbearing and ruled over those he sired with an iron hand, Kir was simply absent. When he was staked just a few years after making Saint a vampire, it meant little since he'd not seen him after being released from his control only months into his new life.

He'd tried to be different with his vampires, but the scars left by his choices ensured that even when he was near them there was a distance that arose from simply being him. More of that penance for what he'd done.

Saint covered his eyes with his forearm and cursed the ability of vampires to remember. How much easier his existence would be if he could forget.

Forget them.

This place.

What he'd done all those years ago that had made him into the creature he was today.

Forget *her*.

3

Solenne struggled to keep her anger in check, but Saint's words repeated in a vicious loop inside her head as she lay in bed waiting for the last remnants of daytime to relinquish their hold on the world outside. Over and over, his words were like knives that cut fresh wounds.

Human females to feed from.

In only minutes, she'd be forced out into the early night to find him a woman to take blood from. And likely have sex with. Right in her own house. A human woman over her.

The insult wasn't lost on her, a proud vampire female.

Reluctantly, she slid from the bed and mumbled, "No surprise your own vampires feel no urgency to help their sire."

A quick shower and she was ready to begin her night.

Pimp for Saint.

Then spy on the local Archon.

Solenne studied the face in the mirror as she dried the last of her hair. Young in the vampire world since her siring in 1921, she was still blessed with the looks of a woman of twenty-four, as she always would be. Blue-green eyes stared back at her as her mind drifted back to that night when Teagan introduced her to a world so completely different from the one he found her in. A world battered and broken after the war, France offered little, but what Teagan promised when he offered to make her a vampire gave her hope.

Teagan. The thought of him all those years ago made a tiny smile creep onto her face. What a charmer he'd been! She would have given him the moon and stars if he'd asked. The loss of her sire at the vengeful hands of one working for those bastard Archons made tears well in her eyes, erasing the sweet memory too quickly.

She'd make them pay for what they'd done.

Wiping her eyes, she took a deep breath. Teagan was gone, and she no longer had a sire. No longer had the protection he provided. Sure, she hadn't needed it in years, and it had been a decade since she'd seen him last, but if she'd ever needed his care, he'd have been there for her.

Instead of Teagan, she had his surly brother under her roof who still blamed her all these years later for the rift between him and her sire. And who planned on punishing her while she worked to keep him safe.

As she set off into the French countryside, she tried to put everything about Saint out of her mind. She was helping the Sons because they were the only ones in their world who had a chance at stopping the Archons. If that meant she had to tolerate Saint to honor his brother and end the Archon takeover, then that's what she'd do.

But it didn't mean she'd make it easy on him.

Solenne made her way along the dirt path that led to the village inn determined she'd find exactly what she needed there. Creeping along the side of the stone building, she saw just what she'd come for outside near the garbage cans.

Petite, with enough cleavage showing for any man, one of the inn's maids would be perfect. Solenne watched her, evaluating her appearance. Appealing enough with her dark hair and a decent body, she would probably be acceptable to Saint, even though she was no real beauty. *Too short, if you ask me.*

"It's a beautiful night, isn't it?" she asked as she appeared beside the woman.

"Oui, Madame," the maid answered nervously as she looked around, obviously wondering where her new companion had come from.

"Parlez-vous l'anglais?"

Nodding her head, the woman said, "Oui, Madame."

"Perfect."

Focusing her gaze on the maid's eyes, Solenne set about hypnotizing her. When she was finished, she took the woman's hand in hers and together they returned to the house. Sounds from the sitting room told her Saint was already awake for the night. She led his female to him but stopped short at the sight of him. Wearing only pants that sat low on his hips as he stood making a fire in the fireplace, he looked incredible.

Flustered by the vision in front of her, she turned to the woman and fighting a stab of jealousy she knew was foolish, mumbled, "What's your name?"

Staring blankly, eyes glazed over, she answered, "Marie."

"Marie, stay here."

The woman nodded, and Solenne walked toward Saint. Standing with his arms crossed over his muscular chest, he wore the look of complete smugness on his face.

With tremendous effort, Solenne kept her eyes trained on his face and not on the perfect set of abs just below his forearms that narrowed to a perfect edge just above his pants. Or what stood just below the top of those pants. She'd forgotten how incredibly exquisite his body was and silently cursed his obsession for working out.

Couldn't have a pot belly. Of course not.

He looked so good she had to fight the urge to reach out and run her fingertips over the chiseled flesh that led to the top of his gym pants. His effect on her unnerved her, a fact she saw he knew by the glint in his eyes as he looked down at her.

"As you ordered, Saint. Willing and not a redhead."

The words tasted like ash in her mouth. That she'd been reduced to taking orders from a man who hated her was bad enough, but orders for the human women she was to bring him was almost too much to bear.

Almost. She was stronger than this, though. There was no way he'd ever see how much she hated this.

"I'm impressed, Solenne. I thought you'd give me a hard time."

What she wanted to give him was a strong slap across the face.

"I'll leave that up to other women. Ones who possess free will, unlike Marie there."

An almost imperceptible wince marred his expression for just a second, and Solenne knew her words had hit their mark. The look of satisfaction that had been in his dark eyes when she'd approached him was gone now, and he quickly directed his attention toward Marie.

"At least she's not a redhead," he said in a flat voice.

Solenne fingered the ends of her own hair at his second snide comment about its color and forced a smile onto her face. "Have some class and keep your activity to your bedroom, Saint. And please clean up any mess you make. My job here is to keep you safe, not to be your maid."

Before he could answer, likely with a painful barb, she turned on her heels to head to her second distasteful chore for the evening. As she walked past Marie, she yelled back, "I'll be home before dawn."

NEVER HAD she wanted to escape her home more than on this night. Even hanging out with those sterile Archons would be better than being subjected to knowing Saint was feeding and making love to some human female in her own house. Looking up, she watched a falling star streak across the sky. Whispering into the darkness, she wished on it. "Let me be strong enough to endure this."

There were only two Archons for all of France—one for Paris and one located in Avignon for the rest of the country. As was the case in other countries where there were so few Archons, both French Archons' offices were a bureaucratic mess, inundated with far too many cases for just two officials to handle. What made the judicial system in the vampire world almost ineffective worked to Solenne's advantage. Eager for any help, the Avignon Archon willingly took her up on her offer of assistance without a thorough background check that may have revealed her true identity. A well-crafted lie about her sire and she was in, able to spy on the very vampires she sought to bring down.

She'd chosen this particular Archon not only because of the ease of worming her way into his circle but also because he was one of the most influential Archons. Far more interested in power than meting out justice for the many petty offenses his office was forced to handle, Marc Verrater made certain he knew the most important goings-on in their world. And he had a penchant for bragging, a reflection of his own self-importance and a habit that had been helpful to Solenne in her job as spy so far.

In minutes, she'd travelled the distance between her home in Valence and the Archon's office in Avignon and was ready to do as she did each time she was forced to spend time with Verrater.

Grin and bear it, knowing she may some night hear something the Sons could use.

Compared to the beautiful old city of Avignon, with its stone fountains and medieval fortress walls, the Archon's offices were nothing less than spartan. Bright white walls and white tiled floors made the place seem more like a hospital than the vampire version of a regional courthouse.

Solenne reported in with his assistant, a plain female named Rochelle who Solenne was sure was the most boring vampire she'd ever met. A pretentious know-it-all, she droned on continually about subjects no one cared about and routinely made mention of how Avignon was famous for being the place of a second home for the Pope in addition to Rome in the Middle Ages. Her act as the local tourist board was boring the first time. Succeeding times made those who came in contact with Rochelle almost universally grow to despise her.

"Good evening, Rochelle," Solenne said, hoping the officious woman didn't take the pleasantry as an invitation to a conversation.

"Lena, how are you tonight? I hear we're in for exceptionally cool weather this week. Terribly odd considering our location. Do you know the average temperature in Avignon in late February is nearly fifteen degrees Celsius?"

Solenne fought back the urge to roll her eyes. "That's nice. Is Marc in?"

Bobbing her head up and down, Rochelle pointed in the direction of his office and began to ramble. "Yes, yes. He just got in. Told me he has some big news. I bet it's about the one who's marked now. I hope he gets some recognition if he's instrumental in getting him. I think Mr. Verrater deserves some. He does so much for the vampires in this country and never gets even a pat on the back. Don't you think?"

God, she was insufferable!

Coming up for air, she took a gulp from her can of diet soda and continued. "He told me when anyone showed up to send them in immediately."

Solenne flashed her a phony smile and walked toward the Archon's office thankful for a reprieve from Rochelle's blathering on. One knock on his door and he was eagerly urging her to come in.

Marc Verrater sat behind an all-glass desk, the kind that screamed minimalist design and a total lack of history or style. The Archon looked nothing like the sterile vampire he was required by law to be, however. His dark hair was cut short, and its color seemed to draw attention to his dark blue eyes. Solenne had never seen anyone—vampire, human, or anything else—with eyes like his. Untainted by any color but the darkest blue, they were mesmerizing even without the effect of a hypnotizing chant.

His body had surprised her the first night she met him. She'd expected him to be like the other Archons she'd encountered, thin and almost sickly looking, but Marc was nothing like that. Nearly as well-built as Saint, he looked physically every bit as powerful as he truly was in their world.

"Lena, come in. Did you see Rochelle on the way in?"

"Yes, sir. Did you want to see me?"

"I do. I'm very thankful for your help. You know, this is a very important time for us."

"Us, sir?"

Leaning forward, he let a sly smile form. "Vampires. It's a very important time to be a vampire. And as an Archon, I have an opportunity to make our world an infinitely better place for all of us."

Especially you and your fellow Archons, I'm sure.

Marc continued on to explain the history of the Archons, how they'd always held a venerated position among their fellow vampires because of the important job they performed keeping order in the vampire world. All of this she'd heard before, but if she ever wanted to find out any secrets to help the Sons defeat these bastards, she had to suffer through his boring history lesson.

"So it's especially helpful that you're here to assist Rochelle with the backlog of cases."

Solenne smiled as warmly as she could muster, hoping to encourage him to continue speaking and possibly give up something useful.

"Anything I can do, sir. She said you had something you wanted to discuss?"

Leaning back in his office chair, he folded his hands behind his head. "Did you hear about the Romanian?"

She'd overheard the jubilation when the news of Vasilije's death had first come in, and now as the Archon spoke of it, her throat felt like she'd swallowed sand. The man sitting in front of her couldn't contain his pleasure at the death of a fellow vampire. Every fiber in her being called out to her conscience to attack the son-of-a-bitch and refresh his memory about the illustrious history of respect Archons spoke of so often.

"Yes, great news, sir," she croaked out.

"It truly was. It pains me, as a vampire, to admit that there are outlaw factions in our world hell-bent on hurting all of us. That he had to be eliminated is a tremendous sorrow to our kind, but necessary if we are to continue to thrive as a community."

"So true, sir."

As the Archon lectured on the idea of community and how each and every vampire needed to be ever vigilant to ensure their world was protected, Solenne sat listening as if a true believer in the cause, almost expecting at any minute Marc Verrater to refer to the vampire world as the Fatherland or something equally as Nazi-like.

"We believe in the greatness of our kind, Solenne. I can see you do too. It's written all over your face."

If she could have, she would have breathed a sigh of relief. There had been times when she'd been sure her utter disgust for the people around her was telegraphed as clear as day by her expression. That Marc thought of her as a kindred spirit in what the Archons were attempting meant she'd be all the more useful to the Sons. Maybe now was the time to probe him.

"May I ask, sir, what of his vampires? I believe he'd sired many."

A sickening look settled into the Archon's features. "Quite true. He'd been a libertine for certain. Siring all those vampires."

Marc lurched out of his chair and began pacing. "As of now, his vampires are of no interest to us. They can't be held accountable for his crimes. Until we determine there is a need to focus on them, they may live in peace."

Solenne wondered what crimes Vasilije was accused of. True, he could be a motherfucker. She'd seen that firsthand in his overbearing treatment of Teagan. That he'd allowed him to move to the States and relinquished control stunned her when she found out. And there were many female vampires who considered him little more than a playboy—a manipulative bastard ruled by his cock. However, none of these character traits added up reached the level of crimes against their kind.

And what had Saint done? Was his transgression simply siring many vampires like Vasilije?

Marc continued his pacing behind her, and Solenne craned her neck to face him as she pressed on in her questioning. "Do you think his death will be a sufficient warning to others?"

Shaking his head, he stopped behind her and grinned

a sadistic smile. "No, we don't believe it will. There are others who have followed the same path as the Romanian. They too must be rooted out if we are to protect and care for our world."

Knowing the answer to her next question, she asked it anyway, needing Marc to believe in her ignorance. "Has there been someone else chosen?"

There was every possibility that he'd find her question too much for a mere temporary helper like herself to ask. Equally possible was the chance that he'd grow suspicious at her increased interest in the workings of the Archons.

But she had to risk it.

Whatever concerns she had about overstepping her bounds were quickly dismissed by the smile that practically lit up the Archon's face. "Yes, another has been chosen. Another who has spent his life dishonoring what it means to be vampire. One named Declan Collins. His assassin has already been arranged and soon he will be just as the Romanian."

The pleasure he found in announcing the impending death of yet another fellow vampire was clear in his voice. It made Solenne's stomach turn, and the taste of bile filled her mouth.

"Already? Has he tracked him down yet?"

Marc leaned in next to her ear. "She, you mean."

"She, sir? Isn't Declan a male name?"

Solenne's question was met with a deep chuckle. "The assassin is a woman. Just as with the Romanian, a female will bring this Declan's time on Earth to an end. It seems only fitting, I believe."

"Yes, sir," was all she could manage to get out before

she felt his mouth on her neck, his fangs sinking into her.

As the Archon pulled greedily on her vein, his hands travelled over her breasts, painfully squeezing her nipples through her clothes, as was his habit every time. Solenne struggled to think of anything but what she would have to endure, occupying her mind with the question of who the woman was who'd taken on the job of killing Saint. Was it someone who knew him? Who could hate him so much as to want to see him dead?

4

"Solenne, can you find a woman who doesn't smell like she's been deep fried in animal fat tonight?"

Closing the door to the refrigerator, Solenne turned to see Saint standing at the kitchen's center island. Shirtless. Again.

"Saint, do you own any shirts, or do you need me to pick some up for you?"

Smirking, he raised his eyebrows in amusement. "Have we become a prude?"

Pushing past him, she sat down at the table and popped a grape into her mouth. "Don't you concern yourself with me, but dial back the Cro-Magnon act, can you?"

Leaning against the counter, Saint propped himself up on his elbows and rolled his eyes. "And the girl from last night?"

Solenne secretly enjoyed the thought of him repelled by Marie for any reason. Maybe he didn't drink from her. That would explain why he was being such an ass. Maybe he didn't sleep with her either.

"Marie seemed perfectly fine to me," she said casually as she picked grapes off the vine. "Maybe you just weren't her type. Maybe she has more refined tastes in men."

"Yeah, that sounds right. A woman who smells like a French fry has refined tastes. Just find me a woman who smells like a woman should."

You'll be lucky if I bring you one at all.

Saint strolled past her after issuing his order as if he were the king of the castle. God, he was infuriating! If she'd ever met a man who could push her buttons more than Saint, she couldn't remember him. Wouldn't have wanted to remember him, at any rate.

It still amazed her how different he and his brother were. Teagan was smooth and so much fun to be around. And Saint? Always the darker, more sullen brother, he'd transformed into a shell of the man she'd met a hundred years ago, more detached and alone than anything else now.

But behind his gruff exterior—behind the defensiveness—that vulnerable soul she'd known then must still exist. At least she hoped it did.

It did no good to think about that now, though. She had a job to do, and at the moment that meant finding a human female to provide him with what he needed.

Even if it felt like she was betraying everything she held dear in her heart the whole time she was doing it.

Solenne sat staring at the book in front of her, stuck on the same page for the last ten minutes. She'd read the same sentence five times and still had no idea what it said.

It was no use. The fact that on the other side of the house Saint and his female du jour, a farm girl named Elise, were together doing something that should be shared by vampires made concentrating on some stupid paperback she's picked up in an airport years ago impossible.

Maybe eating would occupy my mind.

A handful of grapes and a sandwich later and she was no better off than she'd been before. This was torture.

Although she knew she shouldn't, Solenne let her feet guide her to outside Saint's room. Standing there in the hallway, like a masochist desperate for more pain, she listened through the door open just a crack but heard nothing. Heart pounding in her chest, she peered in and filled her eyes with the sight she'd imagined and dreaded.

At the foot of the bed, Elise stood naked and silent as Saint moved his hands over her skin, as if one worshipping a piece of priceless art. Solenne watched in rapt attention as his large hands delicately traced the curves of her body, lingering on the spots that brought a woman the most pleasure. Seated on the bed, Saint gazed up at the human with care in his eyes as he captured a pink nipple in his mouth and sucked gently. When he pulled away, the woman's gentle cries showed her loss.

His hands slid slowly over her stomach to rest on her hips, and he leaned in close to her to press his lips to her skin just above one hipbone. His attention made her arch her back, and in her arousal, she pleaded quietly for him to give her more of what she desperately wanted.

Solenne held her breath, waiting to see more evidence of that man she believed still existed in Saint. The figure so sweetly tending to Elise made her want to believe that vulnerability was still there, buried under years of anger and resentment, but still part of him.

"Elise, I take from you because I must. Take from me."

The tenderness in his words struck Solenne but was replaced by a sharp pang of jealousy that tugged at her deep inside. This woman—this human woman—would know nothing tomorrow of the pleasures she'd receive, pleasures she didn't deserve from one of her kind. That Solenne, a proud vampire female, had not only given her to him but now watched as he made love to her made her cringe.

Was this her punishment for her mistake all those years ago?

Saint's mouth fastened on the female's neck and one sharp cry escaped from her and then she was silent. Her eyes closed, Solenne was helpless to stop her ears from hearing the sensual sound of his mouth pulling Elise's blood into him, the gentle lapping sound of his tongue gliding across her skin as the taste of her blood danced on its tip. The deep, low growl of pleasure from him as her blood slid down his throat, each drop feeding his need for that connection to others.

A connection that should be with other vampires, not those who still lived human lives.

Anger mixed with her jealousy, and Solenne's eyes flew open to see Saint pulling the woman onto his lap. Now he'd fuck her, another act that should have been reserved for those of his own kind. Unable to watch any more of the erotic scene playing out in front of her, she turned away and fled into the night to satisfy her own need for connection.

SAINT HELD the woman to him, her soft body to his hard one, as he took the first of two gifts she'd give him. Her blood did what it needed to do—nourish his soul. Each drop that entered him reminded his body of what he truly was.

A vampire who barely clung to the rest of his own kind.

He'd need the blood of his own soon, though. He could go maybe one or two nights longer, but he needed more than human blood could provide. As it was, he felt himself slipping away from his world, a disconnect born of a lack of vampire blood. If he were to be any good to the Sons, he couldn't let that happen.

If one of his vampires didn't come soon, he'd have no choice. He'd have to feed from Solenne.

No.

Forcing the idea from his mind, he focused on the willing woman pressed up against him. She wrapped her legs around him and pulled him to her, eager for his cock, and he gave himself over to his need to provide some kind of happiness to another being.

Elise stroked his jaw line, gazing at him with a look of curiosity. "Saint? Why would a man like you be called such a thing?"

"A man like me?"

"I've been to church many times, and never once have I seen any saint that looks like you," she said with a devilish smile.

As she spoke, she caressed his back, trailing her hands to his waist and then around to the front to stroke his stiff cock. "And never have I heard of saints being blessed like this."

The feel of her skin on his excited him even more, and the urge to show her exactly how un-saintlike he truly was surged inside him. Fisting her hair, he roughly tugged her head back. "I'm no saint."

Still under his hypnotic control, she whispered, "Show me. Show me you're no saint."

He lifted her off him in one swift movement and placed her behind him on the bed. Turning to face her, he saw her legs spread, her glistening cunt dripping for him. He crawled toward her, his baser animal tendencies ruling him now. Grasping her thighs, he ran his hands up her legs to the sensual vee that was his final goal.

The sultry scent of her sex wafted up to his nose as he dipped his head to her pussy. Musky and sexy, she was just like a woman should be. At the first gentle touch of his tongue to her tender nub, Elise moaned her pleasure.

"More."

Saint flicked his tongue over her clit and slid his middle finger into her slickness. Stroking her tender walls, he slipped a second finger inside her and sucked her swollen clit between his lips.

"More! More!" she moaned as he began to feverishly finger fuck her as he licked her pussy.

This was just the beginning of the more he planned to give her.

Elise writhed under his mouth and fingers as her body raced toward her orgasm. Thrusting her hips off the bed, she ground her pussy into his mouth as she begged him to take her to that point of no return.

The first tendrils of her climax took her over that

sweet edge and as she came into his mouth, her cunt milked his fingers while spasms of pure pleasure overwhelmed her. Saint loved the feel of a woman losing control, her delicious juices running down his chin as his tongue and lips delivered the release she craved. Such sublime happiness was all he could wish for with any woman.

Elise's orgasm and the remnants of it on his lips made him crave more. What his mouth had enjoyed his cock wanted now.

He reared up over her and stared down into her half-lidded eyes. "Now you see what a sinner fucks like."

Kneeling, he pulled her up from the bed and covered her lips with his. His tongue thrust into her mouth, mingling with hers as she rubbed her excited nipples against his chest. Sliding his hands down her back, he squeezed her full ass and pulled her onto his cock. He slid into her to his balls and groaned at how incredible her body felt around him.

"Hold on to my neck and don't let go."

Elise obeyed and soon Saint was like a man possessed, driving into her wet channel to find the perfect moment of bliss for both of them.

"Take me. Make me yours," she begged in his ear as she clung to him. "Make me your sinner."

Her words echoed in his head, transporting him back to a time so long ago when another begged him to take her too. Back to *her*.

For a few sweet moments, the woman in his arms in the present was the only woman he'd thought of for a century.

The only woman he'd ever loved.

Squeezing his eyes shut, he pushed the memory from his mind, but flashes remained. The touch of her hand on his cheek. Her soft hair against his lips. The woman who haunted him.

Fuck. What demon possessed him to bring her back to him? What caused him to be such a man?

Saint shook his head to expel the idea of her from his mind, desperate to focus on the willing one in his arms. Whatever she may have been, human women could provide him with everything he needed.

Almost everything.

Fuck. Saint buried his hand in Elise's hair and tugged with all his strength.

"Harder," she groaned as she bucked against him. "Yes...harder!"

In and out, up and down, he invaded this human woman, searching for that fleeting moment of bliss. He was close, and God help him, he hoped she was. Just a little more and for a few brief seconds he'd be free of the torture of his existence.

Elise's climax won the race over his and just as he clamped down on her neck and the taste of her blood touched his taste buds, her body gave in. Complete and total pleasure flowed from her, taking him too. Together, they shared the fleeting sensation that made him forget everything but the sublime feel of another's ecstasy.

As he held her to this mouth, Elise quietly whimpered her wish to never leave him, but that was just the spell he'd worked. Staying with her, no matter who the "her" was, couldn't be. Saint had accepted that ages ago. Staying meant turning her and once that happened, what they'd just enjoyed could never happen again.

Saint closed the holes in her neck and cradled her face in his hands. Placing a soft kiss on the tip of her nose, he leaned back to study her. She was beautiful with light brown hair, warm brown eyes, and flawless skin. Any man would be crazy not to want to have her every night for the rest of his life.

"Thank you, Elise."

"I don't want to go. Let me stay."

Her brown eyes full of desire stared up at him, and for the briefest moment, he considered letting her stay the night. How wonderful it would be to feel someone beside him as he drifted off to sleep for the day. To hold a woman in his arms for more than sex.

No.

"Thank you for the gift you've given me."

Before she could say another word, Saint began to chant the words that would wipe the memory of this night from her mind. A few minutes later, he was dressed, and she was asleep in his arms as he carried her to the sitting room and Solenne.

"Time for her to go home." Saint placed her in Solenne's arms. "Take care of her."

"Of course. Your wish is my command."

The tartness of her words made it quite clear his wish meant nothing to her. Not this one or any other.

"Just do it, Solenne."

Alone, he returned to his room, but lying around watching overnight television wasn't what he needed. What he needed was something to take his mind off the realities of life.

Solenne's gym was basic, but it would do. As long as he could take the edge off, he'd be able to focus. Being cooped up in Solenne's eighteenth-century country house prison was beginning to take its toll. And she was doing her best to add to the misery.

Twenty minutes on the treadmill only made him wish he could run free through the French countryside instead of in a room forced to face a blank wall. It was unnatural to keep a vampire trapped like this.

Fucking Archons.

And where the hell were his vampires? Did a sire have to be a complete tyrant to receive help? By rights, they should have come as soon as he'd called them. That's how this whole sire thing was supposed to work.

Fuck them too. They have no idea how much they'd miss the freedom I've given them.

The realization that his past hadn't finished haunting him yet pushed him on for another half hour of running, the need to punish others morphing into the need to punish himself. His feet pounded into the rubber of the treadmill and his thigh muscles burned as he ran faster and faster toward nothing and away from everything. Sweat poured from him, soaking his back and chest. It ran into his eyes, blurring his vision and forcing him to squeeze them shut.

Every muscle in his body reacted to his punishment, used to his self-imposed torture and almost taunting him toward more. More punishment. Eventually more pain.

But never more of what he so desperately wanted. Never more of what he needed.

Peace.

Forgiveness.

Only inside himself would he find these, but years

since everyone else had moved on, he still hadn't forgiven himself.

Or her.

Exhausted, he hunched over the equipment, catching his breath. No closer to focusing on anything but the memory that haunted his every waking moment, he relented and let it consume him, unable to fight it.

More painful than anything he could devise as punishment, his thoughts of the past numbed him to the presence of an unnoticed audience to his usually private penance.

5

Vasilije watched in disgust as Saint attempted to recover from the physical beating he'd forced on his body. He'd only watched for a minute or so as the fellow Son nearly ran the treadmill into the ground, but that was more than enough. Just watching it was exhausting.

"Fuck. Is that what you have to do to keep yourself looking like that? That looked like the least pleasurable thing I've ever seen."

Saint's expression at hearing his words told Vasilije that his time with Solenne had done little to improve his disposition, and his response reinforced the observation.

Lifting his head, he snapped, "What the fuck are you doing here?"

"Delighted to see you too, Saint."

Pushing past him, Saint nearly knocked Terek and Solenne over in his hurry to get away.

"Wait, Saint. We need to talk," Vasilije called after him as the three followed him up the stairs to his room where he'd already stripped naked and stood holding only a towel in front of him.

"No, we don't. I need a shower. I have no idea what you or they need."

"Just give us a few minutes, and then you can have your shower. We need to talk about your feeding."

"My what?" Saint's eyes flashed his growing anger at their presence.

"Your feeding. Solenne says you're refusing her blood and only taking human blood."

Vasilije felt Saint's rage explode off him and take up all the space in the room. Solenne must have sensed it too because she took a small step back away from him and stood near Terek.

"Saint, we need you as strong..." Vasilije began.

One giant step brought Saint within inches of his face. Standing toe-to-toe with him, Vasilije stared into eyes full of fury.

"What you need to do is stay the fuck out of my business."

Saint shot Solenne a look of cold hatred and Vasilije continued, hoping to diffuse his obvious anger with her. "Solenne didn't say a thing until I asked, knowing your reputation."

"Vasilije, what I choose to put into my body is my concern. Don't make me tell you this again."

Saint threw his shoulder into Vasilije's as he silently stormed away toward the bathroom, flashing Solenne another look of hatred as he left the three of them standing in his bedroom.

Solenne's expression showed the pain inflicted by Saint's venom. Dropping her gaze, she stared at her hands and then looked at Vasilije, forcing a smile onto her lips.

"I'm sorry, Vasilije. I haven't been successful in bringing him around, even though I've tried to do everything I can to make him happy here."

Terek stepped close to her and gently touched her shoulder with his fingertips. "Don't give up, Solenne. Some men just take longer to come around. He will. Just give him time."

"He's right. Saint is just more difficult than most. Has he had any vampire blood in the time he's been here?"

Shaking her head, Solenne grimaced. "No. Only human blood. I don't know how he does it. He's only a few years older than I am, and I'd never be able to exist on their blood alone."

"He's done it for a long time," Terek said. "It's who he is."

Vasilije nodded. "That may be true, but we need him strong for this fight. Solenne, we need you to keep offering him your blood. Now more than ever, he needs it."

Solenne let out a heavy sigh and said quietly, "I will."

"Let us know if you make any progress. With any luck, Saint will come around. But we've got bigger problems with Ramiel and Thane we need to get back to," Vasilije said, thinking out loud.

As she led them out, Solenne said, "I wish I knew something, but Verrater has never mentioned anything about the prophecy. I guess that's not surprising. So far they seem to be playing this whole thing as them ridding our world of vampires like you."

A sheepish look came over her face and she shook her head. "Sorry. That came out wrong."

Vasilije laughed at the verbal mistake. "It's no problem, pet. Of course they're going to claim I was a degenerate. They can't very well announce that their plan is to kill off the Sons. It's been a long time since most vampires have heard of us, but they'd have a hard time understanding why the Archons want one of the two most important groups in our world eliminated."

Terek added with a smile, "If you're a degenerate, I can't imagine what I'd be considered."

"You keep your vampires—at least some of the females—together with you. I've never known anyone who faults you for that...well, other than why you'd do it in the first place."

Vasilije was one of those who wondered why he would choose to keep what amounted to a harem. Maybe it was from his time with the Arab trader who sired him. Whatever the reason was, Terek was almost a god in some quarters of the vampire world. He, however, couldn't imagine keeping so many of his around.

Terek smiled at Vasilije and bowed slightly toward Solenne to signal it was time to go.

"Solenne, take care. Let us know if you find out anything at the Archon's."

Recovered from the earlier ugliness with Saint, she looked at them both and smiled sweetly. "I will. Hopefully, I can find something to help our cause."

Following Terek into his office, Vasilije was pleased to find Sasa and most of the other Sons waiting for them.

He hoped the sight of Ramiel and Thane away from their books and ancient scrolls meant they'd found something. Anything would be welcome news.

Sasa stood from behind his desk to let him sit, but he waved her off. He liked how she looked in his chair.

"Vasilije, we just heard from Nico. He says the Order of Macaria is safe for now and offers anything it can do to help."

"Any chance they have the answer to this secret prophecy puzzle?" Sion asked. "Our friends here could use some help."

Vasilije sat down in a leather chair next to his desk, unhappy that the news from Ramiel and Thane wasn't good. "I can assume from Sion's question that you're no closer to the answers we need?"

Both males shook their heads. "No. And unless we get a break, we may not be any help at all," Thane said in a voice that showed his disgust for their lack of progress.

"I thought we had something earlier, but it's all just fucking riddles on top of more riddles," Ramiel said as he leaned back in his chair. "How the hell are we supposed to know what those ancient ones meant?"

As they all sat silently thinking about Ramiel's question, Dante entered the room looking like he'd just awoken. Or maybe that was how he intended to look, Vasilije thought.

"What are we talking about?"

"Nice of you to join us," Vasilije said, hoping the young vampire sensed the irritation in his tone. Lately, it seemed the youngest Son was absent far too often.

"Sorry, guys. It's a bitch being a clyten. When your bodies tell you it's time to sleep, mine's telling me to wake up. You try to get used to being a vampire who can walk in the sun."

"I'm quite impressed that we have one of you among our ranks," Terek said as he extended his hand to shake Dante's. "Unique talents occasionally take time to become part of us."

Dante took a seat next to him and put his feet up on Vasilije's desk. "Thanks, man. I appreciate it. Now what are we talking about? Saint hasn't gotten himself staked, has he?"

"No. We're talking about the progress we're making on the prophecy," Sasa answered before Vasilije could.

"Nothing yet? You two aren't relying on those dusty old papers only, are you? It's the twenty-first century."

"Any time you want to leave behind your walks in the sun and join us downstairs, smartass, you're welcome to come. But it's not like you can just Google 'ancient vampire prophecies' and it all comes up on the screen," Ramiel said, allowing the group to see the full extent of his frustration.

Dante turned in his seat to face Ramiel and with a nod of his head said, "Chill, dude. I was just asking. You don't have to get all bent out of shape."

Ramiel was out of his seat at the words "chill dude" and in front of Dante looking like he was ready to release some of his pent-up anger all over the young vampire's face. "You keep this frat boy attitude up and the only thing that's going to get bent the fuck out of shape is you. I don't care what kind of special talent you have or why the Order wants you here."

Terek placed a hand on Dante's shoulder as he moved to confront Ramiel. Dante seemed to quickly understand fighting with the largest Son would be a mistake. Silently, Vasilije wondered if it would be such a bad idea to show Dante his place, but Ramiel definitely shouldn't be the one to do it. A vampire that big and legendary for his violent streak could easily do serious damage to the only one of them who was useful in the daylight.

"Sorry. I meant no harm."

Ramiel scowled and nodded as he turned away from Dante. "I'm out. I need to feed, and this place is starting to drive me crazy. Be back later."

They all watched him leave, understanding how he felt. The monastery was home to Vasilije, but he knew even Sasa felt trapped there sometimes.

"He'll be okay," Thane said quietly. "Ramiel is one of those who needs to blow off steam more often than the rest of us."

"Has there been any progress? Maybe I can help. I'm considered rather logical," Sion said in his stiff manner that made him seem almost robotic at times.

"I wish logic would help. These ancient texts seem to have no rhyme or reason to them. If anything, they seem to be the opposite of logical."

Sion smiled the way he did whenever someone claimed something lacked logic, as if such statements amused him. "I can't imagine the ancient Greeks were so illogical as to put prophecies in writing that made no sense. Let me examine them and perhaps I can see reason where you two can't. Anything is better than spending my time dismantling and reassembling Vasili-je's appliances."

Vasilije looked toward Sasa, who scowled and shook her head, as she clearly sensed how he felt about Sion's tinkering with everything electrical after finding the dish-washer in pieces the day before.

"The rinse cycle seems to be supercharged now," Sasa said with a smile as Sion and Thane left.

"Fantastic," Vasilije muttered. "Don't encourage him. Next, he'll be taking apart the car."

Winking, Sasa smiled. "Yes, love."

"Vasilije, how's our boy Saint handling his new home?" Dante asked.

"Giving Solenne a hard time. He hasn't had any vampire blood since he's been there."

"None? Still doing the human thing?"

Terek answered the young vampire's question. "Our friend just needs some time. Saint is dealing with something only Vasilije can understand. To know that someone intends at any moment to end your life isn't easy."

Vasilije thought back to the vision of Tatiana's seething hatred as she tortured Sasa and then tried to stake him.

"And Saint must deal with his past everyday, a past I doubt any of us really know," Terek continued. "For everything each of us has done, only Saint has been shunned."

Dante dropped his feet from the desk and sat up in his chair. "What did he do? Stake someone?"

Vasilije wrestled for a moment over how much to tell Dante, sure Saint wouldn't appreciate him knowing of his criminal past. The fact was, though, that Dante was part of the Sons of Navarus as much as Saint was and deserved to know who he was working side-by-side with.

"I don't know everything about his shunning, but I

know he was convicted of dishonoring the sire-vampire relationship."

Dante looked at Terek and then back at Vasilije. "For going with humans?"

"No, that began after his time away from our world. That I do know. I knew him in his first years as a vampire and he didn't do the human thing then."

"Then what did he do to get shunned? Christ, you basically have to be public enemy number one to be shunned."

Vasilije knew no more than he'd said, even though he'd asked Teagan right after it had happened. Saint's own brother could only say he'd done something to dishonor the sire-vampire relationship.

"I would assume, then, that it had to do with his relationship with one he'd sired?" Terek said.

"That would make sense. Not one of his vampires has come to his defense, have they?" Dante asked.

Shaking his head, Vasilije said, "No. Not yet."

Each night that passed with no word from any of Saint's vampires made Vasilije wonder if any would ever answer his call. Their refusal—or was it disinterest?— spoke volumes about his relationship with those he'd brought into their world.

"Saint's a lot like his sire. Kir never felt much for those he turned. It wasn't who he was. But Saint's not Kir. He's more emotional, so it's odd that he isn't close to any of his vampires," Vasilije remarked.

"Not even the ones he sired before being shunned?" Dante asked.

"Saint didn't sire until after his time out of our world."

All four sat quietly until Dante asked what had more than once occurred to Vasilije.

"I don't mean to be an asshole, but why was he made a Son? You've got hundreds of loyal vampires, Terek has even more who would walk through fire for him, among his other talents. Ramiel and Thane are important because of the prophecy. Sion has a brain like a computer and vampires who help when called. I can walk by day, and Nico is one of the oldest vampires not in the Order. All of us have something we bring to the table, but Saint brings nothing. He's a criminal whose vampires couldn't care if he's dusted. Why was he called by the elders in the Order?"

Vasilije looked over at Terek and saw in his eyes he'd wondered the same thing. Saint was an incredible fighter and even though they'd had their share of differences, he was one of the few in their world he'd want by him in a battle. But others seemed to possess far greater gifts and they weren't chosen to be one of the Sons.

"The Order chooses those of us they believe can protect them and our world best," Terek said. "While we may not recognize Saint's worth, the Order has and as one of us, we owe him our allegiance."

"I didn't mean anything like that. It just seems that whatever Saint is that made the Order want him..." Dante let his sentence remain unfinished.

"Sometimes what makes someone special can't be seen on the outside, Dante," Sasa said. "Unless I told you I was an empath, you'd probably never know. Maybe it's the same for Saint."

Dante nodded and smiled. "You're right. I was just being stupid."

Standing up, he turned to leave. "I think I'll go grab a bite to eat before I find Sion. We've both got our vampires coming tonight."

Terek waited for Dante to leave and said to Vasilije, "I know what you're thinking, but he's young. And just as with Saint, the Order wouldn't have chosen him if he didn't show promise."

"What he has is the ability to walk in daylight. Other than that gift, impressive as it may be, I'm unsure he has even the common abilities Saint possesses. Being a clyten and having some loyal vampires may be all Dante has."

"Since clytens are rare in our world, that may be all he needs. With guidance, he can be as great as others of his kind."

"Or he may remain reckless. Have you ever met a clyten vampire older than a century, Terek?"

Shaking his head, he answered, "No, but how many former monk vampires do you meet?"

Vasilije smiled broadly. Terek was certainly one-of-a-kind. "I can't say I've ever met any other than you."

Terek's green eyes seemed to sparkle at the comment. "And vampire empaths?"

"I get the point, but just who do you plan to guide him? Are you volunteering for the job? He needs someone to make him into that great vampire you mentioned."

"Perhaps that's my role in the Sons. Only Nico and Ramiel are older, but Nico isn't around and Ramiel's busy at the moment. Plus, he definitely lacks the patience necessary to tutor a young vampire like Dante."

That was certain. Their first lesson would likely be their only lesson, ending with Dante in pieces.

Vasilije turned back to take Sasa's hand in his. For as patient and wise as Terek was, Vasilije didn't envy his challenge of guiding a young vampire like Dante. He'd seen his fair share of his own vampires through their impetuous early years and thankfully now that he had Sasa, those times were over.

"I hope you're up to it, friend."

6

Saint stared out into the moonless night, disgusted by Vasilije's visit. He was used to the sideways glances and snide comments about his preferences from his fellow vampires, but from the other Sons? Of anyone, he thought at least they'd see past his habit.

Who the fuck are they to pass judgment? And who are they to stick me in this fucking house with her to babysit me?

Anger bubbled up inside him at Solenne's part in this. Like a fool, he'd let the very beginnings of trust begin to grow for her. And now the proof of who she truly was couldn't be more obvious.

His jailer.

"Fuck that," he muttered and stormed out of his room, determined to show them all who he truly was. If she planned to stop him, she better hope Ramiel was nearby because he wasn't going to be held prisoner in this place anymore.

Saint found the rest of the house deserted as he made his way to the front door. A twinge of disappointment flickered inside him as he looked back to see no sight of Solenne before he headed out into the night. It would've felt good to blow off some steam before he left.

The cool night air sent a shiver up his spine. How long had it been since he'd searched for blood for himself? Alina. And that had been back in Romania. Well, it was time he got back to acting like a vampire instead of Vasilije and Solenne's too easily caged pet.

Inhaling deeply, he enjoyed the earthy smell of the countryside, but it wasn't long before the memories associated with that sweet fragrance—memories of Teagan, of Solenne, of times he thought would never end—reared up in his mind.

This place was pure torture. When he'd left all those years ago, he'd sworn to himself he'd never return. Now, here he was, Teagan gone, and the woman who'd torn them apart dictating his every movement.

Saint saw the golden light of a candle in the window of an inn up ahead. Like a beacon guiding him to what he craved, it offered the building's invitation to stop and enjoy the night, and he willingly accepted. As he entered, his eyes scanned left and right across the main room, and in seconds he'd found what he desired.

She sat alone at a table near the large, open-hearth fireplace, and in the dim light he saw her expression was one of innocence and what looked like sadness. Her lips turned downward, pushing her perfect mouth into a frown. She looked like she might be waiting for someone as she glanced timidly around the room.

As he walked toward her, Saint examined her more closely, finding the rest of her as pleasing as her pouting mouth. Blonde, petite, and blessed with curves exactly where a woman should possess them, she'd be precisely what he needed tonight.

Lost in thought and staring at the empty seat across the table from her, she didn't hear him approach. For a moment, he reconsidered what he was about to do, noting her sad expression, but Saint put the thought out of his head. They'd cheer each other up.

"Are you alone?"

The woman looked up, her soft blue eyes full of surprise for just a second before they became just as sad as her expression. "Yes," she admitted quietly before lowering her eyes again.

Saint sat down in the chair meant for some neglectful lover and smiled at the sweet face across from him. Who had left this beautiful creature all alone in this country inn? Some young man too stupid to understand her worth or too greedy to accept what she offered, preferring to seek out more erotic tastes before settling down with her? A married lover unable to escape the confines of a cold marriage bed? Whichever it was, their misfortune would be his pleasure tonight.

"What's your name?"

She looked up at him and a tiny smile crept onto her lips. "Janelle. What's yours?"

"Sai... Declan. Nice to meet you, Janelle. What fool has left you alone here tonight?"

"No one," she said, dropping her gaze.

Saint lifted her chin with his forefinger and saw blue eyes staring innocently up at him. She was exquisite, like a doll, and his body reacted to the sweetness he felt from her.

"He's a fool and you shouldn't be sad he stayed away.

Any man that would leave a beautiful woman alone on this night deserves to lose her."

A broad smile came across her face. "It's okay. He was all wrong for me anyway. Married men never leave their wives, do they?"

"Rarely. But now that you're free from him, you can join me for dinner."

"I wonder how smart it is to have dinner with a strange man who doesn't seem to know his name. Or is it that you too belong to another and are lying about your name, Sai...Declan?"

Her teasing tone was charming, and without hesitation, he explained, "My name is Declan, but I have a nickname some use. Saint. I'd prefer you call me Declan, though."

"Are you Irish, Declan? You don't sound it, but with a name like that, I'd definitely guess Irish."

It had been years since he'd thought of himself as anything but vampire. "No, not Irish. I assume you're French with a name like Janelle?" he teased.

Nodding, she chuckled. "Yes, I am."

An hour later, after a very satisfying meal and equally enjoyable company, Saint was ready for what he'd broken out of Solenne's home for. But he didn't want Janelle hypnotized. He wanted her just like she was.

"Let's leave. It's a beautiful night for a walk."

Janelle seemed to consider the reality that it was dangerous to go walking at night with someone she'd met just an hour earlier, and Saint prepared with disappointment to speak the words that would guarantee her agreement. He was happy to see her finally nod her head and smile her agreement.

They walked along the quiet country road, and Saint listened as Janelle talked about living on a farm nearby and her desperate desire to find a life more exciting far away from there. Each moment he spent with her made him wish he wasn't who he was. If only he was the benign stranger she believed him to be. If only he could be the man to whisk her away from the sleepy French country-side to give her that life she longed for.

But that man no longer existed. He had, though. He'd even made a pledge to another beautiful French girl to show her all the wonders the world had to offer. And he would have moved heaven and hell to give her everything her heart desired.

"Do you ever dream about being someone else, Declan?"

If ever there was a loaded question.

Saint stopped next to a lamppost and turned Janelle to face him. In the pale light, he saw her look of surprise when he opened his mouth and slowly lowered his fangs.

"You have no idea how often."

She remained silent, but her gaze never strayed from his fangs. Finally, she looked up into his eyes and asked, "Are you going to kill me?"

Saint shook his head. "No."

"Is this why you approached me at the inn?"

"Yes." This was only partially true. He'd wanted to fuck her as much as he'd wanted her blood, but even more he'd wanted company.

"So the stories about vampires are real. They drink human blood, but they don't kill?"

He was probably the last one who should be acting like a spokesman for all vampires, but he nodded and explained, "Yes, we're real. Most vampires drink the blood of other vampires, actually. And the killing thing varies."

"You don't drink human's blood?"

"I do, but most vampires prefer the blood of our own."

"Why do you drink from humans?"

Explaining that could take hours.

Janelle wrinkled her nose. "I guess if I tried to run you could catch me?"

"I could, but I won't. If you want to leave, I'll walk you home. It's dangerous for a woman to walk alone in the dark."

Smiling sweetly, she said, "Declan, you're not what I'd expect from a vampire."

"Maybe if I had a cape? I don't change into a bat either, though."

His attempt at humor was met with a tiny laugh, and Janelle's eyes scanned his face. "What's it like?"

"Being a vampire?"

"Yeah. What's it like? Do you have to stay out of the sun like the stories always say?" As she spoke, her eyes zeroed in on his teeth again. "Does it hurt?"

"For a moment, and then it fades away."

"What happens when you have blood? Do you turn into a...a monster?"

Saint took her by the hand and began to lead her toward a darkened area off the road. "Come with me. I promise you're safe."

Under a tree, he gently pushed her against the trunk and leaned down next to her ear. "It will hurt at first but hold onto my neck. I'll only take a little."

Janelle whispered her agreement. "Okay, but if I ask you to stop, will you?"

"Yes."

Years of experience told him she wouldn't want him to stop, but if she did, he'd respect her wishes. He pressed his lips softly to the tender spot below her ear and closed his eyes. Her skin was warm and soft and held the faintest scent of lilacs. Slowly, he dragged the tip of his tongue over the spot where he'd pierce her skin and heard her sigh in anticipation.

Gently, at first, he pushed his fangs into her tender skin and felt her grasp at his neck. Just a few seconds more and the pain would be replaced by pleasure. Her blood hit his taste buds, and Saint felt something like an electrical current run straight from his mouth to his cock. Something about her willingness to trust him made the experience all the more sensual and his body yearned to enjoy the rest of her.

Janelle's hands loosened their grip on his neck, and she let out a tiny moan as he began in earnest to take her blood into him, breaking his promise to take only a little. That demon which silently ruled him—greed—took over, and Saint felt his will begin to slip away.

As he'd expected, she begged him not to stop as her hands sought out his already rock-hard cock. With each pull on her vein, she stroked the hardness through his pants, nearly driving him over the edge. Her moans grew louder, and she ground her pussy against his cock.

This wasn't going to end with a mere taste of her blood.

Saint tore his mouth from her neck and looked down into her eyes full of desire. "Tell me what you want."

Her words made his cock jump, eager to fulfill her

every wish. "Make me forget my life. Show me you'd never leave me alone in some inn."

Saint hurriedly peeled her dress off, revealing a pink bra and panties that just as quickly found their way to the ground. Janelle eagerly worked to undress him and when he lifted her to him, she wrapped her legs around his waist and pushed her wet pussy against his cock.

"I wanted to fuck you the moment I saw you, " he groaned as the first inches of his cock slid into her cunt.

"Yes...more," she moaned as he eased his full length inside her. "Fuck me, Declan."

Turning her away from the tree, he began pumping into her looking for that moment of bliss her body would give. She was tight, her channel a perfect fit around his cock. Each thrust in and glide out of her body touched nerve endings that made him almost lose control.

Janelle's tongue followed the motion of his cock as she played with his tongue and fangs while she bucked her hips to meet his thrusts. Hoping to prolong the pleasure, Saint lowered himself to the ground and laid back in the cool grass beside their strewn clothes. Still inside her, he stilled a moment to look at the woman on top of him.

Blond hair tumbled over her shoulders and breasts and her pale pink nipples stood proudly waiting for the touch of his hands or lips. He slid his palm over her soft skin at her hip, over her ribs, and cupped a full breast as he gently pinched her excited nipple. Moaning, she squeezed his fingers tighter on the pearled skin and rocked her hips back and forth against him.

He pulled her down to him and as she rode him with abandon that signaled her release was near, he whispered, "I want the taste of you on my tongue when you come from my cock inside you."

"Yes, take from me," she whimpered breathlessly into his ear.

Rolling her over onto her back, Saint pumped into her, his cock like a perfect fitting addition to her needy cunt. She grabbed his ass and pulled him into her as she met each of his thrusts with one of her own.

He felt her body begin to close in around his cock and knew she was only seconds away from release. Sinking his teeth into her neck, he pulled on her vein and just as her body began to spasm around his, he got lost in the taste of her blood on his tongue.

Her orgasm seemed to go on forever, and she cried out her ecstasy as he felt the first of his own explode into her. The rest of the world fell away as they enjoyed one another's pleasure, each taking and giving equally. The bliss he sought in sex didn't disappoint, and for one long and beautiful moment, he was happy, his past didn't haunt him, and he believed he deserved both those things in his life.

Janelle kissed him sweetly as she cradled his face in her hands. "Declan, thank you for the most incredible time I've ever had. And for making me feel sexy again."

"It was my pleasure."

As much as he wanted to stay there, lying in the damp grass with this beautiful creature in his arms, he knew this was impossible. He risked being seen by one of the Archons' henchmen, and no matter how much happiness making love to Janelle had brought him, he needed to return to Solenne's.

When they arrived at Janelle's house after remaining

silent on their way there, she took his hand in hers. "Will I ever see you again?"

"I don't know," was all he could say.

The answer was no, but he didn't want to hurt her feelings. Sex with her had been incredible, and Saint was sure few women tasted as delicious, but if he saw her again he'd want to turn her and once that happened, everything good would be lost.

"Do you have someone?"

Saint shook his head and kissed her softly. "No. I have no one."

Janelle touched his cheek and smiled. "Strange. You act like a man who has someone at home. She's one lucky lady, whoever she is."

As he watched her safely go inside, Saint wished what she'd said was true. The thought of having someone still crept into his mind, no matter how many times he'd chased it away as an impossibility. But like all those other times, he once again told himself that desire was one he'd never enjoy.

Saint hoped he'd be spared a confrontation with Solenne when he returned to the house, but that wish remained unfulfilled too. He'd barely made it through the door before he saw her. The saying "If looks could kill" ran through his mind at the sight of the anger written all over her face.

"What the fuck do you think you're doing?"

"Definitely not the way a man wishes to be welcomed home, Solenne."

Saint walked past her to the kitchen and prayed she

wouldn't follow. Like his earlier wishes, this wasn't to be either. Perhaps the time had come to clear the air.

"You could've been attacked. Did you forget the Archons have targeted you now?" she asked in an exasperated voice from behind the refrigerator door.

"I didn't forget, Solenne. I just got tired of being locked up. I wanted to go hunting for myself."

As he stared at the condiment bottles on the top shelf, he waited for Solenne's response, but there was only silence. Had she walked away, leaving their inevitable confrontation until another time? A quick glance at the floor to see her black boots told him no. He wasn't going to get off that easy.

Unsure of what he'd find, he stood up straight and closed the door. He was ready for her anger, but the hurt look on her face surprised him.

"You're a real asshole, Declan."

With that, she turned and walked away, leaving him with the insane need to confront her. So now he was Declan? He hadn't heard that name from her since the last day he'd seen Teagan, and she thought she could remind him of that time without having to deal with the repercussions?

No fucking way.

He stormed after her and caught up with her in the hallway to her bedroom. Grabbing her arm, he spun her around to face him. "You don't get to use that name. I didn't ask to be stuck here with you. If you have a problem with what I did tonight, I can be out of here before dawn."

"Stuck here with me? Like anyone else would have you. There's a reason none of your vampires want to help you. Maybe if you didn't prefer humans to your own kind, someone other than me and the other Sons would care if you lived or died!"

Her words were like razor blades cutting into his skin. Fuck her and her words! "I prefer humans because..."

Before he could finish, she cut him off. "You prefer humans because you don't have to do any work for them. And your refusal to take what you need from me is going to hurt you and the rest of the Sons, you selfish prick!"

Solenne turned to walk away, but something snapped in Saint. He grabbed her by the shoulders and pushed her hard into the wall. "You want to help the cause, sweetheart? Fine. As you wish."

Saint's fangs snapped into place, and as Solenne struggled against his hold, he dropped his head to her neck and sunk his teeth deep into her skin. Tugging roughly on her vein, he savored the taste of her blood more than he wanted to admit. Every inch of his body was on fire, and memories of the past flooded into his mind, nearly knocking him off his feet.

This was why he preferred human blood—any blood —to hers.

7

The feel of his lips pressed against her skin and the sensual tug on her vein as he drank her blood overwhelmed Solenne, and she pressed her thighs together tightly to stop her impending orgasm. Her body's reaction to him surprised and embarrassed her, and when he stumbled back against the wall, she turned her face to avoid meeting his gaze.

How was it possible that after all these years and everything that had happened he could still have an effect on her?

Saint made a noise like an angry growl, and she turned to see him leave without another word. Had the taste of her blood repulsed him so much that he had to flee from her? Or was it possible that he'd felt what she had?

Exhausted emotionally and physically, all she wanted to do was climb into bed and curl up under the covers away from the world. Away from Saint. But she was already late for the Archon because she'd waited for Saint to come home. God, he was going to drive her mad!

Even though she knew she had a responsibility to get to Verrater's office tonight, she didn't want to leave without at least trying to make peace with Saint. There would be none, though. His door was closed, and he was holed up in his room. Peace would have to wait.

It was probably better that she kept her distance anyway. With the effect he had on her, who knew what could happen if she went into his bedroom.

SOLENNE ENTERED the Archon's office and immediately sensed something significant was occurring this night. Rochelle was practically shaking from excitement behind her desk. Only the arrival of someone important or a new development in the case against Saint would make her all aquiver.

"Rochelle, what's going on? You look like you're about to burst!"

The secretary flailed her hands near her hair that resembled mousy brown cotton candy and breathed so heavily Solenne was afraid the woman might pass out before providing the answer.

"Oh, my! It's so exciting! The one who's been chosen to do the job on that Declan fellow is due here at any moment."

Solenne's heart pounded so hard against her chest it hurt. Why on Earth would the assassin be there unless they knew Saint was hiding in the area? Somehow, she had to get back to the house.

"Wow, that is exciting! But I think I'm feeling a little

under the weather tonight. Maybe I should go home."

From behind her, Solenne heard Marc Verrater's voice. "You must stay tonight, Lena. We have an honored guest with us. I'd like you to meet Emily Tarnen."

Turning, she saw them, and Solenne extended her hand to shake Emily's, noting how small her hands were. "It's a pleasure, Miss Tarnen."

"She's the one to kill the newest vampire chosen, Lena."

Emily Tarnen was practically beaming at being introduced as Saint's assassin. Solenne knew no matter how much she wanted to get home she needed to stay right where she was.

"Oh, thank you, Mr. Verrater. You're too kind."

"Remember, call me Marc."

"Yes, of course, Marc," Emily cooed.

The Archon's gaze never wavered from the girl, and Solenne fought the urge to recoil from Emily's sugary-sweet voice. She sounded like she was perpetually stuck in time as a cheerleader.

"Rochelle, hold all my calls. Lena, join us. I may need you to take notes."

Solenne looked at Rochelle's crestfallen expression and weakly smiled her apologies for Verrater's obvious slight as she followed him and Emily into his office. As she entered, she spied his hands linger a moment too long on Emily's shoulders as he helped her remove her coat. More and more, Marc Verrater seemed far less like what an Archon was supposed to be and far more like the vampires he persecuted. Not that his admiration wasn't reciprocated. Emily was clearly infatuated with him, a powerful and attractive man paying attention to her.

Solenne felt almost as if she'd intruded on a private moment and moved to back out of the room.

"Lena, come," Verrater said motioning with his forefinger to indicate where she should sit for their meeting. "Sit down and listen to what Emily has to tell us."

Emily turned to Solenne, eager to explain why she'd be willing to murder a fellow vampire. As she began to tell her story, her brown eyes appeared to almost dance, as if the reasons behind her hatred of Saint brought her some measure of happiness. While she spoke, Solenne studied her. She looked rather average, overall, with plain brown hair that fell in waves to her shoulders, and there was nothing unique otherwise about her face or body, as far as Solenne could see.

But somehow Saint had found a way to offend this ordinary female with the too-sweet voice so grievously that she wished him gone from the Earth.

"Did you have a good sire, Lena?"

Solenne nodded, remembering how wonderful Teagan had been when he'd first turned her.

"You're lucky. I wasn't so lucky. My sire was the worst."

"I'm so sorry."

"He hates our kind. That's why I want to help the Archons get rid of him."

Emily's almost chipper announcement that she would be killing a fellow vampire unnerved Solenne. Saint didn't hate their kind. She didn't know why he preferred human women, but she truly believed it wasn't because he was a vampire hater.

Marc rose from his desk. "I have some business to take care of. You two talk, and Lena, I'd like you to take notes for our files."

"Yes, sir."

He moved around to behind Emily and again his hand grazed her shoulder. Looking up at him, she smiled. "I'll do just as you told me to, Marc."

"Very good. I'll be back in a little while and we'll leave then."

As Solenne readied herself to take notes, Emily's eyes followed the Archon until he closed the door behind him. Alone with Solenne, she was more forthcoming and eager to give more details about her grudge. "Ask me anything, Lena. I promised Marc that I would tell my story to assist him."

Solenne sat straight as an arrow, a notepad on her lap and hundreds of questions in her mind. If she worked this right, she might be able to find out even more than this silly girl intended. Luck was surely with her.

"Maybe starting from the beginning would be best."

"Sounds good." Before she began, she popped a stick of spearmint gum in her mouth and chewed it until it was soft enough to crack. "Well, my sire's a vampire named Declan, but you already knew that, didn't you? Did you know he has a nickname? Saint. I can't imagine a worse nickname for someone like him."

As Emily ranted on about Saint's nickname, punctuating her points with the loud cracking of her gum, Solenne wrote down everything she said. Little of it seemed like it would be worthwhile to the Archons, and Solenne began to wonder what they saw in this woman to make them think she could be of any help whatsoever.

"How old do you think I am, Lena?"

Solenne smiled fakely. What she wanted to say was that Emily looked about as old as she acted, but saying she was like an overgrown teenager wasn't going to get her anywhere, so she took a guess. "Twenty-three?"

"No, no. I mean as a vampire."

"Oh. I don't know."

"1951."

Touching her sleeve slightly, Solenne said, "You're still a youngster. I'm so jealous!"

"Oh, you're so sweet! I feel like a hundred years old lately. If I had a sire who wasn't a criminal, I know I'd feel so much better."

Solenne grasped her hand and gave it a gentle squeeze. "I'm so sorry, Emily. It's just so awful. Are you sure you want to talk about it? I'm sure Mr. Verrater would understand if we waited for another day."

"Thank you, but I want to continue. Talking about it helps. Where was I? Oh, yes. 1951. Well, he attacked me and turned me into a vampire without my consent or anything. It was terrible!"

Solenne patted her hand and smiled sympathetically, but each word she spoke convinced her that Emily was lying. Saint was many things, but a brute who committed what equaled to rape in the vampire world wasn't one of them. True, consent wasn't necessary when one chose to turn a human, but he wasn't the type to attack anyone.

"Where did this horrible assault occur?"

"New York. I was a young, innocent girl working as a receptionist at a record company. One night I was on my way home to my house in Queens and he set upon me like the monster he was!"

Emily began rooting through her purse and Solenne made sure she committed the details of what she just claimed to memory. New York. Queens. Attacked. Her notes were far more extensive, of course, since Emily seemed quite interested in reading them as she dabbed her eyes with a tissue.

"Are you sure you can go on?"

Sniffling, Emily nodded and continued dry-eyed. "So there I was, a vampire with this strange man who was supposed to take care of me. But that didn't happen."

"He didn't refuse to feed you, did he?" Solenne asked in the best horrified voice she could muster.

"No. He did something far worse. He was a sex fiend! All the time, day and night. When I said no, he forced himself on me. It was dreadful. Rape! That's what it was."

Solenne prayed her face showed none of the thoughts running through her mind. So this was what the Archons were using to justify Saint's murder? That he was a sex fiend and rapist?

This made no sense. Why portray him as an over-sexed sire when the truth would be as offensive to many of their kind? That he chose to sleep with human women made him a traitor to the vampire race in more radical circles. Why not use what he really was against him? Few others in their world, outside of the Archons, disapproved of a sire's sexual behavior with his or her vampires, and to most, it was a perk earned by a sire for adding to the shrinking ranks.

Emily continued on with her act and Solenne wrote down every salacious detail, but her mind was focused on how she could get home to talk to Saint and the rest of the Sons. Maybe they'd understand why the Archons had chosen to construct such an elaborate tale with someone she suspected had never even met Saint.

By the time she'd finished, Saint had been branded a

rapist many times over, a vampire who kept a corral of females at his beck and call to service his constant need for sex, and Emily had used half a pack of tissues drying tearless eyes.

"Is there anything I can do? I feel so terrible you had to endure something like this," Solenne said as she leaned in to hug her.

"No, but now you know why I want to help the Archons rid our world of such a monster."

Marc returned just as Solenne broke the embrace and sat down behind his desk. "I hope you were able to take down everything, Lena. It's such a powerful story, isn't it?"

Unlike earlier, his focus was squarely on her, and the power of his stare unnerved her. "Yes, it is, sir. Appalling is how I'd describe it."

"Rochelle said you weren't feeling well earlier. If you're still feeling under the weather, just leave your notes with her on your way out and she'll take care of them. You and I will resume our work together the next time you're here."

Solenne flinched at his reference to the work they would resume next time, but she tried to focus on being able to speak to Saint instead. "Thank you, sir. I do feel quite sick to my stomach."

Turning to face Emily, she said, "It was a pleasure meeting you, Emily. I admire your courage. Will I see you again?"

"Thank you, Lena. I don't know, but once the world is rid of that monster, I hope Marc will allow me to come back for a visit."

"I'm sure that would be delightful, wouldn't it, Lena?"

"Yes, sir."

The Archon's focus was once again on Emily, and Solenne felt increasingly uncomfortable, as if she were in the middle of the first moments of their foreplay. As she left, she sensed they didn't even notice she was gone.

Solenne dropped off her notes with Rochelle and watched her pour over them as if they were gospel. Before she was forced to endure any more which might make her truly sick, she begged off and left as quickly as possible.

SAINT STOOD in the doorway of the sitting room eating a sandwich and watching something about Jack the Ripper on television. Solenne was surprised to see him fully dressed, including a shirt.

"We need to talk, Saint."

"Yeah, about before..."

No, she definitely didn't want to talk about how he'd run from her after tasting her blood. "No, not about before. We need to talk about what's going on with the Archons and you. I'll get Vasilije and the others on the phone so we don't have to do this twice."

As Solenne walked down the hallway toward her room, Saint yelled, "What's happened now? Change their minds?"

Not exactly.

Back in the sitting room, she dialed Vasilije's number. "Think the opposite."

"They want to make me an Archon? Sorry, but I'm about four hundred vampires past that," Saint said with a chuckle.

"Stop joking around."

Vasilije's voice on the other end of the line interrupted their verbal sparring. "Solenne, what news do you have?"

She looked at Saint's face and smiled. "Do you have any idea why they'd want to make anyone think Saint's a rapist?"

Saint's eyebrows raised in astonishment. "What? Now I'm a fucking rapist? Who am I raping?"

Vasilije tried to calm Saint down. "Relax, Saint. Solenne, what are you talking about? Saint's no rapist."

"I know that, but I just sat through a meeting with the Archon and some woman who claims Saint's her sire and he was nothing short of a sex fiend with his female vampires, even forcing them to have sex against their wishes."

The line went silent, but in the background Dante could be heard laughing. Finally, Vasilije asked, "Are you sure you're not mistaken, Solenne?"

Saint's expression showed he was as confused as Vasilije was. "Solenne, who is this vampire of mine?"

"Does the name Emily in New York City in 1951 ring any bells?"

Saint shook his head. "No. I've never been to New York."

"Vasilije, they spent a lot of time making Saint out to be the worst of our kind. Any idea why his preference for humans shouldn't be enough justification for the Archons to get rid of him?"

"Solenne, I'm worried they know about you. And they know about us."

Staring at the phone, Solenne was silent, understanding the importance of Vasilije's words. If the

Archons knew who the current Sons of Navarus were, then they planned to pick them off one at a time. It wasn't a coincidence that both Vasilije and Saint had been targeted.

"Are you saying you don't want me to go back to the Archon's?"

"I can't tell you we don't need you to continue spying on him, Solenne. I just can't say I'm sure you're safe anymore," Vasilije said somberly.

For all the horrible things she'd endured at the hands of Marc Verrater, she still believed she could be more helpful to the Sons and Saint if she continued spying on him. "I understand, but I can handle myself, Vasilije."

"Okay, but if you sense you're in danger, you need to get out of there, pet. I don't want to see you get hurt."

"Vasilije, if they know about us, then none of us are safe. I'm coming back tonight."

Saint's eagerness to leave after she'd just said she would risk her safety for him and the Sons stabbed at Solenne, but she pushed down the hurt to focus on the problem at hand. "Vasilije, what do you need me to do now? I'm not scheduled to go back to Verrater's until tomorrow night."

"Keep up what you've been doing and help Saint with his needs there. Saint, we can't risk the Archons finding you along with Ramiel and Thane. Stay where you are, but be careful."

The scowl on Saint's face said more than any words, and Solenne again cringed at the pain of his unhappiness at being with her there.

"I'll let you know if we find out anything here, and

Solenne, call immediately if there's any news from the Archon. Saint, be safe."

"Vasilije, wait. Has there been any word...anything from any of my vampires?"

The line fell silent for a long pause. "None yet, Saint. But they'll come. Give it time."

Saint hung his head and sighed. "Yeah."

SOLENNE SAT SILENTLY REMEMBERING the words she'd said just hours earlier to him as Saint sat down heavily in a chair across from her and hunched over, his head still hung. She shouldn't want to speak the words that would make him feel better, to apologize for saying what she truly believed in her heart was true, but she also knew she'd hurt him. After everything he'd done, she shouldn't care if he were happy or not.

Watching him there like a man defeated pushed all those thoughts aside, though.

"Saint, I agree with Vasilije. They'll come around. Your vampires just aren't used to you wanting them around."

Slowly, he raised his head and she saw his dark eyes clouded with doubt. "Don't."

He rose from the chair, walked past her, and returned to hand her a piece of paper with an address on it.

"Her name is Janelle. Tell her Declan needs her. Give me a half hour, and don't hypnotize her."

Solenne fought back the tears as his words echoed in her ears.

Declan needs her.

8

Saint studied the intricate design on the ceiling above his bed. Someone had taken the time to painstakingly form the plaster into tiny swirls that gradually flowed into larger arcs. The whole effect only made him feel worse than before.

"What a fucking waste of time," he muttered. "As if there was something wrong with plain old white paint."

The idea that now he had Vasilije and Solenne pitying him made his stomach turn. Like he needed their pity? Even if none of his vampires came to him, he could handle himself against those motherfucking Archons. He didn't need anyone's help. He'd been practically alone for almost a century. This was no different.

"Declan?"

In the midst of his misery, he looked over toward the door to see Janelle. Like an angel from a fantasy come to ease his soul, she stood in a long white dress, her blond hair framing her beautiful face, and blue eyes full of concern met his.

She was exactly what he needed to make him forget the reality of his world.

He sat up and waved her in to sit next to him. "Come in. I'm glad you came."

Janelle sat beside him and with a look of worry studied him. "That woman said you needed me. Is everything all right?"

"Everything's fine. I just wanted to see you again."

Without a word, she touched his cheek, stroking it tenderly with the pad of her thumb. Her skin was warm against his and each touch made him want more of her.

"Declan, who's that woman? She's obviously not a sister, but I'm guessing she's like you? A vampire?"

Closing his eyes, he let himself enjoy the sound of Janelle's soft voice, even if the words she spoke only served to keep his mood foul.

"That's Solenne. She's a vampire. She was my brother's vampire."

"What do you mean she was your brother's?" Janelle asked as she let her finger slide down his jaw.

"My brother was her sire—he made her a vampire."

Saint opened his eyes. Janelle sat staring at him, looking as if she were trying to understand what he'd said, "So she's sort of like a sister?"

"Not exactly. At one time she would have been more like a sister-in-law, but now, no."

"Why did she tell me you needed me?"

"Because I do."

Saint pulled her to him and kissed her hard. In some way, he wanted her to feel what was eating him up inside without having to tell her. He didn't want to have to speak the words because to say them would be like torture.

Somehow, if she could know without him having to feel that pain, he could feel better.

Janelle's kiss aroused him just as it had before, and in seconds his cock was rock hard. Her lips were so soft against his, like warm silk, and her tongue playfully sought out his, inching his desire up notch by notch as she sweetly feasted on his mouth.

Breaking the kiss for just a moment, he leaned back to look at the woman who would once again give him the gift of those few precious seconds of happiness. Maybe she could be more. He enjoyed being near her, and she seemed to feel the same for him. Could she be what every one of his vampires never had been?

For the first time in years, he believed he could be the kind of sire he never was before.

Janelle opened her eyes and looked up at him. "Declan? What's wrong?"

Shaking his head, he smiled and placed a kiss on the tip of her nose. "Nothing's wrong. You make me feel happy."

Grinning, she slid her hands over his chest and stomach to just above his pants. "Good. Is part of that happiness biting me?"

"Definitely."

Janelle began undressing him and roamed her hands over his skin, enflaming every place she touched. As she gazed at his body, she whispered, "I shouldn't be okay with that. I know. But there's something about you that makes me want to do..."

She broke off her sentence to place a kiss near his collarbone and then looked up at him and whispered next to his skin, "...bad things."

Her breath was warm and light as it drifted across his chest. With her lips, she delicately teased a trail over his pecs and abdomen, stopping where her hands had earlier. Ever so lightly, she skimmed her fingers under the waist of his pants, grazing the tip of his cock.

Her touch. Her words. Saint closed his eyes and let the happy feeling wash over him. "Declan, let me make you happy."

Janelle opened his pants, and Saint let his head loll back when she wrapped her hand around him. God, it felt so good! Slowly, she stroked him, her hand sending waves of pleasure through his cock and balls.

Just when he was convinced he couldn't feel better, her mouth closed around his cock and her tongue slid over a spot just beneath the head, sending pleasure radiating throughout his body. Looking down, he held his breath at the sight of Janelle's perfect mouth and hand stroking his shaft.

Then, out of the corner of his eye, he spotted a figure peering in through the cracked door. For a moment his eyes locked with blue-green eyes, and he felt their pull on him. Eyes filled with an all-too-familiar anguish held him hostage, their pain squeezing his heart like a fist jammed in his chest.

Janelle dragged her nails over the skin of his inner thighs, sending excitement racing to his balls again, and Saint closed his eyes in ecstasy. In the darkness, the woman just outside the door was there, her gaze fixed on him with a woman.

A human woman.

Damn her! Why should he care that his time with any

woman pained her? What right did any vampire female have to pass judgment on him for anything?

That he'd let that happen once before in his life was a mistake he swore he'd never make again. Ten years as an outcast, branded a criminal, had made him who he was. Ten years, every day a reminder that he was unwelcome in the world of those he loved. Every day his heart squeezed in a vice of solitude.

Every day haunted by betrayal.

Saint opened his eyes and shot his gaze toward the door, but there was no one. Was his mind playing tricks on him?

He was a fool if he let Solenne's disapproval spoil his chance for happiness.

"Janelle," he groaned as her mouth inched him closer and closer. "Come to me."

Pulling her body tightly to his, he slid his hands over her beautiful ass and squeezed. "Give me what I need."

Standing in front of him, she slowly slid her dress down her body until it pooled at her feet. There, in the moonlight, she looked like a goddess, her blond hair shimmering in the soft light of the evening, her body his to worship.

Saint's eyes feasted on her beauty as his hands traced the seductive outline of her body. Full breasts, tender and soft to his touch, rose and fell under his attention. A tiny waist flared to a woman's hips. Janelle sighed as he caressed his touch over her soft skin.

"Declan, take what you need."

He pulled her onto his lap and felt her slick pussy glide over his cock. Excited, she moaned his name and wrapped her arms around him, clinging to his neck. "I want you inside me."

Her words enflamed his desire as much as the feel of her body against his, and he rolled her onto her back to take her. God, he wanted this! To be inside her, her body, his body taking and giving until neither knew where one ended and the other began would make everything else disappear, at least for a few moments.

Hovering over her, he let his gaze travel over her pale skin so similar to one of his kind. Beneath him, she arched her back to touch her body to his. So sweet, so willing.

The thought of turning her burned in his brain as he slid his cock into her wet channel. Each thrust into her made the idea something he didn't want to dismiss with his usual excuses.

Perhaps he'd found the woman who could make him forget his past.

The feel of her hands holding him to her—needing him—filled him with joy. While he could turn her if he chose, a willing partner would mean far more to him.

"Janelle," he whispered as he stilled inside her. "Stay with me."

For a second she was silent. Had she understood his meaning?

Wrapping her legs around his waist, she held him tightly inside her. "Declan, take me. Make me your vampire."

The thrill of her words shot through his body, and his fangs slammed into his mouth. It had been years since he'd sired a vampire, but instinct surged in his veins, and the need he fought every night took hold of his very being. Like a creature with a singular purpose, he sunk his teeth into her neck and drew her warm blood into his mouth.

"Oh, Declan...this feels...don't stop," she whimpered as he took everything she was into himself. "Make me yours for every night."

Every night. She would be his to take care of every night. He would do it. Finally, after all those years, he could be a proper sire.

Don't do this, Declan.

Saint's eyes flew open and with his mouth still on Janelle's neck, he darted his gaze left and right to find the one who'd said those words, but he saw no one.

Only a minute more and she'd be ready. But the words echoed in his mind. *Don't do this, Declan.*

Was he going mad? Had being cooped up in this house finally driven him insane?

He knew whose voice haunted him. Her next words stopped him dead. *You can't be what she needs. She'll grow to hate you like all the others. You know your fate. Accept it.*

Saint sat bolt upright, expecting to see Solenne standing next to his bed, but there was no one. With sadness, he looked down at the nearly turned Janelle lying silently next to him, her eyes closed. All it would take was a few more tugs on her vein and she'd be one of his vampires. Someone to devote himself to, protect, and care for.

Someone to end the life he'd led for so long.

Her blond hair lay spread out behind her head like a halo of an angel. He softly traced her delicate features as he tried to convince himself Solenne's words were lies, but as blood fell from his lips onto Janelle's cheek, marring her beauty, he knew the truth.

As he wiped the crimson drops from her skin, he knew he couldn't be the sire she needed. Bending down, he placed a small kiss on the lips that had brought him such happiness. "I'm sorry, Janelle."

For a long time, he lay next to her, listening to the gentle beat of her heart grow stronger as the minutes passed. He'd missed the feel of a woman by his side in bed more than he wanted to admit. Thousands of empty days alone should have rid him of the memory, but they only served to sharpen it and the need for that feeling to return to him once again.

Saint felt the dawn approach and carefully dressed Janelle. Silently, he bid her goodbye and took her into his arms before carrying her out to Solenne. She looked up at him, her blue-green eyes showing her confusion at the look of rage he knew he wore. He couldn't conceal it. She'd stolen another happiness from him, and he hated her for taking Janelle from him.

"Take Janelle home."

Solenne stood and looked first at the woman in his arms and then up at him. "Is something wrong?"

Shaking his head, he fought the urge to let his rage explode out of him. "No. Do what you're supposed to do and take her home."

She took Janelle with no argument, and he watched as she walked toward the door with all his hopes in her arms before disappearing into the night.

· · ·

THE HOUSE SEEMED SO empty now as he sat and stared blankly at the TV. Soon it would be time to hide from the day, but for now he was content to just close his eyes and attempt to forget all he'd wanted from Janelle.

"Saint?"

Solenne lightly nudged his shoulder, and he opened his eyes to see her seated next to him with something in her hand.

"What time is it?"

"I don't know, but the sun has been up for a while."

Scrubbing his hands over his face, he tried to wake up. "I must have dozed off."

"I wanted to show you this. I found it the other day when I was putting away some of Teagan's things."

Saint looked down at what sat in her lap. A program from some show, it instantly brought back memories that had been silent for decades.

"Do you remember when the three of us saw those dancers? I'd never laughed as much before in my life."

"Don't, Solenne."

The joy in her eyes faded to sadness. "Why?"

"I can't do this with you."

The tears in her eyes forced him to look away, but he couldn't escape her words. "I miss him. I miss thinking about him from all those years ago. You're the only one in the world who can truly understand my loss."

All he could do was shake his head. No words could convey how true her statement was. He did understand her loss. He'd felt it since hearing about Teagan's death, but he couldn't do this. Not with her.

"Saint, I know you miss him. Why can't you just say you do?"

Turning to face her, he saw the tears on her cheeks. "Why? What good does it do?"

"We shared so much then. Maybe our memories can keep him alive in our hearts."

"I don't need any more memories keeping any more things alive."

"He was my sire. I can't just let the memory of all he was to me then fade away to nothing. I need those memories. How can you just let all that fade away? He was your brother, no matter what happened."

"I can't think about the time we spent together, Solenne. It comes with too much bad."

Solenne hung her head and tears dripped down onto the program she held in her hand. "I can't be in this house with you like this. I made mistakes. I admit that. Am I never to be forgiven?"

"Did he forgive you?"

Lifting her eyes, she smiled as she wiped the tears away. "Yes. But that was never the problem. I was his vampire."

"You were more than his vampire, Solenne. You were his."

"One of many. We were young. I grew to understand what kind of man he was when it came to love."

Saint studied the woman in front of him. Her barely veiled justification of her actions bothered him, and her ability to move on felt like it was undeserved.

"So he forgave you and you've rationalized that since he went through women like water that what you did was okay? Have you rationalized everything about your past away?"

Solenne frowned and shook her head. "No, but I won't

apologize to you when I wouldn't to him. I never meant to hurt him, and he understood that. I paid more than you know for my mistake."

"How nice for both of you."

He'd heard enough. Apparently, only he couldn't put that past behind him. So be it. As he rose to leave, Solenne took his hand in hers and gave him that look that never failed to make him weak.

"Forgiveness isn't an end, Saint. It's a beginning."

9

A smoky haze hung heavy in the air all around Declan, a combination of the remnants of the day's battle and the encroaching night air. The pitted ground beneath him, hard and full of jagged stones that stabbed his lower back, had been his home for hours after he'd fallen in the early afternoon of the battle. Around him lay many of those who'd charged on the German line that morning, so full of life and now dead or waiting for their final moment when the excruciating pain of their wounds would finally relent.

The wailing sound of agony had filled his ears all day as one by one fallen men of the 36th Ulster Division went to meet their maker. He'd gotten it in the shoulder, the pain making him lose consciousness almost instantly, but he'd held on long enough to find Teagan, who'd been at his side when the charge began. Now as night began to fall, he felt the end coming closer and needed to know if his younger brother would soon join him.

"Teagan, talk to me," he groaned to the body near him.

"Declan, did we get any of those fucking Krauts?"

He had no idea if they'd had any success after they'd been thrown back by a vicious German counterattack. If the number of bodies littering the field around him was any indication, their effort had been a failure.

"Yeah, we got them. The 36th showed them what us Irish lads have in us."

Teagan groaned as if the Devil himself was standing on his injured leg, and Declan saw the pain written on his face when he rolled over to face him.

"We're going to die here, aren't we? I don't want to die in France, Declan."

Declan reached out and held his arm. Where they'd die wasn't going to be of their choosing, but at least they'd be together. He'd promised his mother he'd watch over his younger brother when she'd sent them off to fight the Germans, and he'd lived up to his word.

At least there was that.

That she'd lose both her sons on this godforsaken field in northern France wasn't a choice any of them would've made. He'd never wanted to fight this or any other battle, but like every other soldier who'd signed up to stop the Germans, he knew he had to.

"Don't talk about dying. We're not dead yet."

"They're going to leave us here, Declan. We're never leaving France," Teagan whispered, his voice full of the anguish his brother acutely understood.

Eyes closed, he silently agreed. Quietly, he said the first lines of the only prayer he could remember at that moment.. "Our Father, who art in heaven, hallowed be thy name..."

Teagan let out a cry of pain and Declan opened his eyes to see a man crouched down next to him. His jet-black hair hung in front of his face as he seemed to examine his brother, but he was no medic.

"Get your hands off him! Don't touch him!"

The dark man lifted his head and Declan saw his blue eyes look first to him and then past him to someone else. "This one's mine. Will you take that one?"

Declan turned to see a man standing at his side looking down at him as if he were deciding on what to do. Much larger than the man near Teagan, he looked different in appearance too. As if his true opposite, he had pale blond hair and a Nordic look to him.

"Who are you?"

The man answered the dark-haired man's question with a nod and said, "Kir."

A sense of desperation came over Declan as the idea that his brother had already died settled into his heart. "Teagan! Talk to me!"

Silence.

The dark-haired man smiled and lowered his head to Teagan's neck. Declan didn't know if he could help, but he begged, "Save him! Help my brother."

When the man raised his head, Declan saw a pair of razor-sharp fangs dripping with blood. His brother's blood. "I will save him, as Kir will save you. And then you'll have lives others have only dreamed of."

The man returned to Teagan's neck, a vampire who intended to take his brother's life. Everything in Declan raged at the sight of him drinking from his brother. He may have been close to death, but he couldn't let some vulture take Teagan for his own! With his good arm, he struggled to push the man off him, but a large hand restrained him.

"Don't fight this. Vasilije will give him what he wanted—

not to die in France. Something tells me you don't want to die here either, but I'll give you the choice."

What he offered was no choice. Either he died there on the pitted and scarred landscape surrounded by his countrymen, or he became a vampire, dead but not dead.

Declan watched helplessly as the life was drained from his brother. Teagan, weakened from his wound, put up no fight. The dark man stayed at his neck and Teagan grew pale, his eyes slowly fluttering closed. Then the one called Vasilije punctured his own wrist and pressed it to Teagan's pale lips. Declan watched in horror as he eagerly lapped at the blood that flowed from the man's arm.

"Your brother is almost there, Declan. Are you willing to let him go on without you?" Vasilije asked, taunting him.

The promise he'd made to his mother all those months before repeated in his head. In this, he had no choice.

He turned back to Kir, who awaited his answer. "I don't want to die."

"Good. You'll do well as one of us."

Without warning, Kir seized upon him and sank his sharp teeth into his neck. Declan cried out in pain, certain the vampire had betrayed him and intended to end his life, but just as he was sure he could endure the pain no more, something inside him began to change and the pain was replaced with pure contentment.

The injury to his shoulder didn't produce blinding pain anymore and a sense of calm overcame him. Even as Kir drained his blood from his body, Declan felt more alive than he'd ever felt in his twenty-five years.

And then he felt nothing.

He watched as Kir sat back away from him and repeated what Vasilije had done to his own wrist. From what seemed like miles away, he heard Teagan's voice telling him everything would be fine.

Then Kir's cool skin pressed against his lips, and he tasted the thick liquid that oozed from the puncture wound in his wrist. Unlike anything else he'd ever drunk, the blood was metallic tasting and almost sour as it washed over his taste buds. It slid easily down his throat and any worries he'd had about feeling sick from it were pushed out of his mind when the strength that had steadily ebbed from his body all day long surged back through his limbs.

Kir removed his wrist from his mouth, and Declan gasped for air, his first action as a vampire. Next to him, Teagan smiled his usual cocky grin. "You were right, brother. We aren't dead yet."

"It's time we left this graveyard. Come and begin your new life," Vasilije said as he helped Teagan to his feet, his injured leg as healthy as the day he was born.

"I need to stay with my brother," Declan said as Vasilije began to lead Teagan away.

Kir extended his hand to help him up, and once on his feet, Declan examined his shoulder to find it was just as healed as his brother's leg. Something impossible had occurred and he hadn't died.

"Come. I will see if Vasilije will allow you to remain with your brother. You have much to learn and he will help you."

They walked through the field of dead bodies to catch up with Teagan and Vasilije, who had made their way across the battlefield. Declan wondered how they appeared so close so soon, while he and his sire remained as if strangers.

By the time their first night was over, he felt no closer to Kir but distanced from the brother he'd protected all his life, replaced by a new protector.

.   .   .

SAINT AWOKE from a day of dreaming, exhausted both emotionally and physically. Solenne's need to reminisce had made his subconscious work overtime. Maybe she was right. No one else but them shared memories of Teagan like they did.

But that meant they'd have to be willing to put past hurts aside, and he wasn't sure he could do that. Almost one hundred years later, he still wasn't able to leave the past behind.

"I'm bored with Paris, Teagan. Tell Vasilije you want to be let off your leash."

Declan saw his brother roll his eyes at the snide comment about his sire. He knew how he felt about the Romanian, who ruled over his vampires like a tyrannical despot, as far as Declan was concerned. His sire had released him from all but the basic rules of being one of his vampires within months of his turning. He rarely required any contact with him at all, and Declan had become accustomed to the level of freedom Kir provided.

"The women are all the same here. Aren't you tired of every night the same offerings?"

Teagan reclined on a Louis XIV antique sofa and lit one of the Turkish cigarettes he enjoyed. "You say this at least once a week, but you always end up finding something you like."

"I settle for what I need. Don't confuse that with liking."

A voice behind him said, "You are the least fun a vampire can be, Declan."

Spinning around, he saw Vasilije standing in the doorway to the hotel suite the three of them shared. The picture of excess, he appeared as he always did.

Satisfied. Sated.

"Nice to see you, Vasilije. I didn't realize you'd returned." More like he'd hoped he wouldn't. His effect on his brother in the five years since they'd been turned was anything but positive, as far as Declan was concerned. Because Vasilije insisted on having his favorites around, Teagan was required to be with him constantly, except on the all-too-rare occasion that his sire spent time in London.

"I've just come from the club next door, and I can assure you that your assessment of this city's women is incorrect. I met the loveliest American artist and there seems to be quite a few new faces out tonight. So get rid of your glum face and join us."

Teagan was already off the sofa and eager to see what his sire had boasted of, but Declan doubted his claims. He'd seen what Vasilije liked in human women before. As long as they attracted the attention of every male in the room, human and vampire, they were instant favorites. That they rarely had any substance at all seemed not to matter.

"Come, brother. Perhaps tonight will be the night you find a woman you truly like. Not that I understand this need to truly like a woman to enjoy your time with one."

Reluctantly, Declan followed them. "I can't imagine siring someone I didn't like."

Both Vasilije and Teagan stopped and turned to face him. "Kir has given you permission to sire your own vampires?" Teagan asked with more than a hint of jealousy in his voice.

Declan couldn't keep the smug look from his expression. There were benefits to having an absentee sire, after all. "Of course. My sire trusts me."

"Your sire doesn't pay you nearly enough attention. He has no idea what you do," Vasilije chided in a scolding tone.

"Lucky me. When do you plan to trust my brother enough to allow him to sire?"

He knew the answer to this, but they deserved the jab.

"He's too young a vampire yet. There's plenty of time for siring later. Now he should enjoy as many different experiences as possible."

Declan pushed past them on the way to the stairs. "He sounds like a parent or nanny, Teagan."

Behind him, he heard Teagan whisper his reasons why he should be able to do the same things as his brother, who was made a vampire on the same night. Declan doubted he'd make much headway with the Romanian, however. From that first night he'd showed a special preference for Teagan over almost every other one of his vampires. While his brother certainly benefited from his relationship with his sire, often to the extent of making Declan jealous, that closeness had a price.

Declan noticed as he entered the club that Vasilije was closer to being right than usual, even if he'd exaggerated a bit. His American art school student had a bevy of friends who seemed drawn to the three males like moths to a flame. Each one beautiful and charming, they quickly become very pleasurable entertainment for the three vampires. Postwar Paris did seem to have its appeal, after all.

But after a few months of them, Declan had decided none were anyone he wanted to sire. Restless for the chance to experience something other than the Paris nightlife Teagan and Vasilije seemed never to tire of, he began contemplating where to go. Staying with Vasilije and his brother had its perks since it cost him nothing, but the time had come for him to leave.

Declan knocked on Teagan's bedroom door to break the news to him. Alone after a night of debauchery, he lay naked on the king-sized bed looking very much like his sire.

"Teagan, I have something I'd like to discuss with you."

"Come in. Come in. You missed a wonderful party, brother. Did you see the beauty who just left? Fuck, she was delicious in every possible way."

Sitting on the chair near the door, Declan nodded in false appreciation for a women he'd barely noticed as she breezed by him minutes earlier.

"So what do you want to talk about? You look even more serious than usual."

For the first time since that day on the battlefield near the Somme in 1916, Declan felt an emptiness in the pit of his stomach knowing tomorrow he and his brother wouldn't be together. Twenty-five years as a human and five as a vampire had made his decision a painful one. The promise he'd made to their mother rang in his ears, but Teagan had another protector now.

"I've decided to leave."

"No. Why? You live here for free, and Vasilije even gives you blood when you need it. How will you live? Your sire does nothing to help you."

Declan frowned at his brother's inability to understand why the life he and his sire loved left him feeling empty and alone.

"I'm not like you and Vasilije. Fuck, most nights I can't even stand being near him. I want something more than a different woman each night."

Teagan sat up on the bed and slipped on a pair of pants. "What if I ask him if we can go somewhere else? You pick the city, and we'll go. He'll do it. I'll tell him I want it."

"You're not hearing what I'm saying."

"Declan, you can't go. You're my brother."

"I'll always be your brother, Teagan. I don't need to be with you to be that."

"Where will you go?"

"I don't know. Somewhere I can find the life I always wanted before we became this."

"This?"

"Vampire."

Teagan looked at him with a confused expression. "I hope you find what you're looking for, Declan."

A KNOCK on his bedroom door drew Saint from his memories, and he sleepily shuffled across the room to answer it, knowing it was only Solenne. He wasn't sure he could handle much more memories, though.

He opened the door and saw her standing there staring up at him with a look that told him she wanted to talk.

"What's going on, Solenne?"

She took a deep breath and then spoke. "I was hoping we could call a truce."

Saint looked down into those ocean blue eyes gazing up at him and sighed. "I can't fight the Archons and you. I can't do this anymore."

The smile that met his words lit up the room. For the first time since he'd come to her home, she was the women he'd known all those years ago, the woman his brother had sired and cared for.

The woman he'd cared for.

"Saint, I know you've never forgiven me, but I hope we can at least be friends."

"I don't know, Solenne. All I know is that I can't fight

you and the rest of the world anymore. Give me a minute and I'll get dressed. I want to go out tonight."

Disappointment clouded her eyes and the smile that had charmed him just seconds earlier slid from her face. Looking down, she quietly said, "Oh."

He knew what she thought. Tipping her face up toward him, Saint smiled. "I thought it would be nice if you came with me."

"To find you human females?"

"To enjoy dinner."

As if his mere words had lifted her spirits, her eyes grew wide, and her beautiful smile returned. "Oh. I'd like that."

"Good. Give me a few and we'll go."

10

The house rested back from the road, obscured behind the heavy foliage of ancient trees that had watched more than one traveler mistakenly pass by. Made of stone, the house had a subtle warmth from its pale-yellow color that was accentuated by the royal blue farmhouse shutters flanking each deep-set window of the façade. In the light of dusk, Declan imagined it could be a welcome sight to one who'd taken the time to find it.

A row of lanterns above the door and first floor windows illuminated the home and a stone patio near the front door. Wooden chairs and a table placed in the only open spot among all the trees seemed curious for a vampire's house, but a singular lantern in the center of the table alluded to nighttime use.

Stepping up to the entrance, Declan knocked on the old wooden door and waited between two concrete lion statuaries. Nearly a year since last seeing his brother, he wondered how Teagan had found himself in this place on his travels. The house seemed an unlikely place for his brother to land, even temporarily. The closest village almost a mile away seemed an equally sleepy locale when he'd passed through it, utterly incapable of providing Teagan the excitement he craved since his time with his sire.

As he thought with distaste of seeing the Romanian, the door opened and there stood Teagan. As it had always been, it seemed as if Declan was looking in a mirror at an image of himself just one year younger. Brown eyes almost identical to his stared back at him, slightly wrinkled around the eyes from his brother's genuine smile.

"Declan! It's wonderful to see you," he said as he enveloped him in his arms.

It was good to see him too. When they'd parted that night in that Paris hotel suite, Declan had held no hard feelings but questioned if he'd ever see Teagan again.

"This is a beautiful house but a bit off the beaten path for you, isn't it?"

Teagan laughed all the way from his belly and opened his arms wide as he looked up toward the ceiling. "This? This isn't mine. It belongs to one of my vampires."

Declan stopped short and stared in shock at him. Teagan a sire?

Turning back to face him, his brother wore a smile that beamed with pride. "Surprised? Don't be. Vasilije favors me too much to deny me anything for long."

"I thought he'd selfishly keep you as sterile as an Archon for much longer," Declan said, looking around the grand hallway for any sign of his brother's sire as he followed Teagan to a sitting room at the back of the house.

"He's not here, so relax. I didn't want our first meeting again to be marred by anything, so he's off in London."

Teagan seemed different as he spoke of Vasilije now, as if he'd matured from the young man his sire had kept plied with

Absinthe, women, and sex to a man more like Declan himself. He liked the man he'd become.

He took a seat near an enormous fireplace that dominated the room and listened as Teagan talked of his past year, each story full of vivid details and laughter.

"You seem happy, Teagan. I'm glad."

"I bet you're wondering why I wrote you to come visit, aren't you?"

"A little, but just seeing you like this is enough reason."

"Well, I have another. There's someone I want you to meet."

Declan saw by the glimmer in his brother's eye that he was referring to a woman. "Someone? When did you become a one-woman man?" he joked.

Before he could comment on the change, Declan saw the woman he assumed could be given credit for this new Teagan. Very much his style, she was stunning with strawberry-blonde hair, deep blue eyes that reminded him of the Mediterranean at sunset, and a body made for seduction. As he rose from his seat, Declan watched with happiness as she sweetly placed a kiss on his brother's cheek.

"Solenne, this is my brother, Declan. Declan, I'd like you to meet Solenne, the owner of this house and my vampire."

"It's like seeing double. It's a pleasure to meet you, Declan," she said with a smile that lit up the room.

"Likewise," he said shaking her hand. "Your home is beautiful."

"Thank you. It was a gift from a lovely woman who took a shine to me. I hope you'll consider it your home for as long as you stay with us."

Declan watched her, enthralled by her warmth and enthusiasm. Even simply seated next to Teagan, she radiated an energy unlike anyone he'd ever met before. He couldn't imagine anyone not taking a shine to her, and not just for her beauty.

The three talked for hours about everything from the war to the brothers' childhood years in Ireland. When Solenne gave her apologies for retiring early, Declan was sincerely sorry to see her go.

Alone with his brother, Teagan grinned like a schoolboy with a secret ready to burst from his mouth. "She's terrific, isn't she?"

"She is. You're a lucky man, Teagan. New to siring and you've been lucky enough to find her. I hope to have that some-day. Will you ask her to bear your mark?"

Teagan walked over to a cart full of decanters and poured them each a glass of whiskey. "She's great, and we have a great time together, but she's not my only one. I sired a few before her, and I have my eye on one of the village girls. I'm not inter-ested in being saddled by a mark."

Handing Declan his glass, he sat down on the sofa again and took a sip of his drink. Head thrown back, he closed his eyes and inhaled deeply. The scene reminded Declan of that selfish, satisfied look that Vasilije always wore.

Whatever change he'd believed he'd seen had been an illusion. Teagan was exactly who he'd been since that night he'd been turned. Jealousy surged in Declan's chest. His brother had what he'd always wanted out of life—someone to love and to love him back—and it meant nothing to him.

"She obviously cares for you. Why isn't that enough?"

Teagan let another mouthful slide down his throat before he spoke. "Why should it be? I'm crazy about her, but it's not like I was only going to sire her."

The taste of whiskey burned the back of Declan's throat. "Why did you want me to meet her if she's just a lay?"

"It's not a problem with her, so why should it be one for you? She knows how I am."

Shrugging, he asked again, "Why am I here, Teagan?"

"I thought you'd like to see that I'd become a sire."

His brother's words were like punches to his gut. This wasn't about wanting him to meet Solenne. This was about rubbing being a sire in his face. Even though Kir had approved of him siring years earlier, he'd never gone through with it. Nobody he'd ever met seemed right—seemed like someone he'd want to know for the rest of his time on Earth.

And now his brother had sired Solenne and others.

Declan threw the rest of his drink down his throat and stood to leave. He'd had enough of this reunion. "I'm thrilled for you, Teagan."

"Your room is at the end of the hall from our room. Rest up. Solenne wants us all to go out tomorrow night."

Even though he tried not to show his disgust, the sound of his glass slamming down on the table made it perfectly clear. "I don't think so."

Teagan reclined on the sofa, his entire being the picture of smugness. He was enjoying this. "Don't be like that. Solenne's looking forward to it. It'll be fun, and it looks like you can use some of that."

"Good night, Teagan."

Declan stepped out into the dim hallway that led from the sitting room to the main hallway and front door. He grimaced from the stabbing feeling in his chest and hung his head for a moment as his time with his brother replayed in his mind.

No, he wouldn't be staying.

Rounding the corner into the grand hallway, he heard a

voice whisper his name. Turning, he saw Solenne, who stood hiding against the wall, her finger up to her lips.

"I hope you're not leaving," she whispered close to his ear. "He was looking forward to seeing you."

He saw her look of disappointment and leaned in next to her. "I think it's best if I leave." As he spoke, the subtle fragrance of flowers filled his nose, and he closed his eyes to savor it. She smelled like sunshine and summer.

Before he got lost in memories of long, sunny Irish days, he backed away from her, but she caught him by the wrist to stop him. "It's nice to have company. He leaves sometimes for a week at a time. And when his sire comes back..."

Solenne's voice trailed off leaving her thought incomplete, but Declan didn't need her to finish. The look on her face told him she thought of Vasilije much like he did.

"Why don't you leave when he's gone? Does he force you to stay here?"

"No, he's not like that. He's quite free with me as a sire. I just prefer to stay here. I don't like all those parties he attends."

At least Teagan didn't force her to stay at home while he went out hunting for women to sire and fuck.

Looking down into her sad eyes, he said, "I don't belong here. I'm sorry."

As he turned to leave, she grabbed his hand and gently squeezed, her eyes wide and pleading. "Give him a chance. You're brothers. Family should be closer than you are."

Something about the way she looked up at him made his body feel like he was stuck in concrete, even though his brain was screaming the order to run. But it didn't matter. Deep inside, he wanted to give Teagan a chance for them to be brothers again.

.   .   .

"DID YOU ENJOY THE MEAL?"

"I did." Solenne looked around at the people who sat next to them inside the Cafe de Flore. "Why did you want to come to Paris, Saint? You never liked it here."

She wasn't wrong. Just the mention of the name made him think of his days after the war with Teagan and Vasilije. But there were other memories of Paris. Better memories of him with Solenne and Teagan.

"Not always."

They sat in silence as the people around them celebrated whatever had brought them out that night. It was all so relaxed, and after his decision to try to let the past stay where it belonged, Saint wanted to relax.

He knew he shouldn't. The Archons still wanted him dead, and he was still basically trapped in Solenne's Valence home, but for tonight, he wanted to enjoy life.

As he looked at Solenne now, he could imagine her as the woman who'd sat with him enjoying the night air at a long-closed cafe nearby. Her hair was much shorter then, barely reaching her chin, and it always seemed to be under some hat or another.

"What are you smiling about?" she asked innocently.

"Your hats. Do you remember them?"

That beautiful smile lit up her features and if it was possible for a vampire to blush, Declan would have sworn her cheeks pinkened.

"I loved those hats! I was quite stylish in those days. I remember that enormous hat I wore when the three of us..."

Solenne turned her face away from him. "I'm sorry, Saint. I didn't mean to bring him up. It's just so hard."

"I know. Since I found out he was gone, he's been on my mind too."

"If I'd just had the chance to say goodbye, maybe it wouldn't feel like this."

Solenne looked at him, and he knew what she felt. For everything that had happened between them, he was his brother, the last of his family, and now he was gone.

"I don't want the same thing to happen to you. The Archons plan to make an attempt on you soon. They haven't said anything to me, but I feel it. Just sitting here in a cafe like this is a risk, Saint."

"Solenne, I can't stay holed up in your house night after night. I'm a vampire. I need to hunt since I don't have any of my vampires. And I won't live in fear waiting for the fucking Archons. If those bastards want me dusted, I'll go after them instead."

A look of terror crossed her face. "You can't! Vasilije and the other Sons need you. And Vasilije said..."

"Don't bother telling me what the Romanian wants. If I stay, it's because I have a duty to the Sons and the Order to stop those bastards, not because he tells me to."

He knew he shouldn't have been so hard, but he'd spent too much time listening to his brother's sire already. "I didn't mean to bite your head off. Sorry."

A tiny smile formed on her lips, and she looked down as she began to chuckle. "Do you hear yourself some-times? For someone so serious, you're quite funny. A vampire saying bite my head off."

He smiled in spite of himself, but even more so because her giggling made him want to smile. Sitting there with her at a cafe enjoying a drink, he realized he was happy. Genuinely happy.

It had been a long time.

"I've missed that smile. I know there hasn't been much to smile about so far, but I hope I get to see it again."

"Remind you of Teagan?"

Slowly, she shook her head. "No. It reminds me of Declan."

Saint emptied his wine glass and motioned for the waiter to pay the check. "It's time to go."

IN SECONDS, they were on the other side of France and back at Solenne's house. In the place where the table and chairs had been all those years before when he'd first come to this house stood a bench, and Saint sat to enjoy the cool night air. Mist from the river rolled over the grass, making everything dewy, but he didn't want to go inside yet. For just a few minutes more, he wanted to enjoy his freedom.

"I'll give you some privacy. If you need anything, I'll be right inside," Solenne said quietly.

"No, you don't have to go. In fact, I'd prefer if you stayed."

Without a word, she sat down next to him on the bench. For a long time, they sat in silence, looking up at the starry night sky and the thought occurred to him that he loved this house. Away from so much of the world, it was a sanctuary, not a prison like he'd thought of it. Slowly, what it had meant to him all those years ago came back, and he let the feeling settle into that long empty space in his chest.

Staring up at the sky, he said the words he'd put off

since he'd arrived there. "Solenne, I need you. None of my vampires will help me, and I can't last much longer on human blood."

He deserved a hard time from her. He knew this. Barely a minute had passed before tonight when he hadn't been a prick to her. When she finally turned to him and spoke, it wasn't a hard time he got.

It was worse.

"That's what dinner was about? You needn't have bothered. I told Vasilije I'd be willing to give you my blood until your vampires show up, and the offer's still good. You're no good to any of us if you can't even stand up."

Her cold response made him wince. He deserved that too, but after their time together, he hadn't expected it.

Solenne stood and positioned herself in front of him to allow him to feed.

"No. Sit down," he ordered gently.

"Saint, you need this."

"I do, but my way."

Solenne sat down, and he knelt in front of her. Slowly, he ran his palms up her thighs so her knees fell open. Leaning in, he inhaled the scent of flowers on her skin and his fangs shot into his mouth.

"Solenne..."

His lips touched the soft skin of her neck, and his head began to swim. It had been so long since he'd enjoyed the taste of a vampire female. Anticipation raced through his veins like a drug hitting his bloodstream.

Solenne stroked the back of his head and tenderly pulled him toward her. "Take what you need."

Unlike in the hall near her bedroom, this time he

gently pierced her vein and waited for her blood to touch his tongue. The first taste of her made his cock stiffen, and for the first time in so long, he yearned to truly share himself with a woman.

But that wasn't possible.

He reveled in the strength Solenne's blood created in him. What had been absent from him for longer than he wanted to admit flowed through him now, bringing his body and soul back to life.

He could let himself need this again.

11

The feel of Saint's mouth drawing what he needed from her body thrilled Solenne and silently she pined to feel him inside her. To feel his body invading hers, making her submit to his long-denied needs. Desire coiled inside her driving the urge to feel him under her fingertips. Trailing over the soft hair on his head, her touch elicited moans that vibrated against her skin.

He was so powerful between her legs, his body pressing open her thighs as she struggled to close them to fend off the orgasm that would be proof of her desperate longing for him. His chest pressed against her, forcing her nipples to sensitive peaks, just more of her that craved his touch.

As if to torture her, he kept his hands motionless on the tops of her thighs, and with each pull on her vein, she prayed he'd move his hands to touch her anywhere. Fear of his response kept her still until she could bear it no longer, and slowly she inched forward to feel his body fully pressed against her. She didn't care anymore if he knew how much she wanted him.

Her pussy ached for the touch of him, and with the last scoot of her behind forward on the bench, the wet juncture between her legs made contact with his hard abs. A deep groan escaped from between his lips and reverberated against her neck, and for the first time he moved his hands, pressing firmly into her flesh near her hips.

His fingers were so close. Just a few more inches and he'd give her what she'd waited so long for. What she needed so badly she'd risk the humiliation of rejection once more for the slimmest chance that this time he'd let her in.

The pull on her vein grew weaker, and she held him to her never wanting their time together to end. She felt him push against her hands and reluctantly she slid them over his shoulders as he raised his head to face her.

Please don't pull away from me.

Through closed eyes, she sensed his gaze fix on her. If she never opened them, maybe this moment would never end.

In a husky voice she imagined he'd use as he lay next to her after claiming her in every way a man could possess a woman's body, he whispered, "Look at me, Solenne."

Tears burned her still-closed eyes as the fear that he would now yank her out of her fantasy back into the cold reality of what they were gripped her heart. The gentle touch of his hands as he cradled her face gave her hope, but still she couldn't look at him for fear the moment would be crushed beneath his words.

"Look at me, Solenne. I need you to look at me."

She raised her eyelids slowly and in the pale light of the moon he knelt looking up at her, his dark eyes as gentle as she knew they could be. His face, which so often had shown the hard lines of his nature, appeared softened and kind. If only his words were the same.

"Thank you. I hadn't realized how weak I'd become until I felt your blood inside me. I'd let myself forget what strength feels like. You gave me what I needed."

Words bubbled up inside her, mixed with the joy at hearing his words. She wanted to tell him she'd longed to see this side of him, free of anger and resentment. To see the man she knew all those years ago. Instead, she pressed her lips together so as to not ruin the moment.

And then he leaned in toward her. Tilting his head, he stared into her eyes with a look of longing, and his lips met hers in a whispersoft touch that made her heart ache.

"Sire?"

The voice of a female behind him broke the spell, and they both looked to see a young woman with long, dark hair looking down at him.

"Sire? I'm here to answer your call."

Solenne watched in disappointment as Saint stood and moved away from her toward the stranger. One of his vampires had finally answered his summons, and what she'd given him just minutes earlier would no longer be needed.

"Maria."

He seemed surprised by her appearance. Or was that relief she heard in his voice?

"I knew you'd come."

Saint turned back toward Solenne and introduced her to his vampire. "You're saved from having to deal with me anymore," he joked.

"What do you mean?"

"You won't have to put me up here now. Maria can give me what I need so you don't have to be bothered."

"You're not leaving. You can't. Vasilije and the other Sons need you safe," Solenne stammered out as her head began to spin and her heart pounded wildly. Was she expected to just let him go with some strange woman who seemed to have suddenly appeared from out of nowhere?

But she wasn't some stranger. She was one of Saint's vampires come to give him what he needed like any good vampire did for their sire.

"I'm sure we can find a room in the village. I'd hate for us to put you out," Maria chimed in.

We.

Us.

You.

Her words rang in Solenne's ears.

Solenne watched as Saint's vampire urged him to leave with her at that moment, tugging his arm like a child urgently wanting to return home. Before she could convince him, Solenne had to stop him. Touching his other arm, she whispered close to his ear, "Can I talk to you over here? Alone?"

Relieved for the moment by his willingness to listen to her, she led him to under the trees and away from Maria. He looked down at her as if he couldn't imagine what objection she could have to his leaving.

"Saint, I don't feel good about this. Stay here with Maria. Please. You're both welcome in my house."

Just saying the words made her feel like her heart was being ripped from her chest. She didn't want to beg, but she would if she had to. Whether she was merely jealous or it was something else, she couldn't let him leave.

"Don't worry. She's one of mine, one of the few I was sure would come. We'll just be in the village."

"But what if the Archons move against you?"

"I'll have Maria's blood to keep me strong. Don't worry."

Saint turned away from her, but in desperation she grabbed his wrist and he turned to face her, his look one of surprise. "Please, Saint. Do this for me then. Please."

He stared down at her for a long time and then smiled. "Okay. If it makes you feel better, we'll stay."

Solenne watched as Maria reluctantly agreed to her sire's wishes. Very young in her ways, she seemed especially eager to be alone with him. If her sire were anyone other than Saint, Solenne wouldn't have thought twice about it. But her sire was a vampire known for his refusal to sleep with any female of their kind.

She followed them inside wondering if she was simply being jealous. Maria had, after all, interrupted what she'd waited so long for. And the ease with which Saint had abandoned their intimate moment stung. Just watching him lead Maria toward his room, his hand tenderly placed on the small of her back to guide her, made Solenne's chest hurt.

Will this torture ever end?

There was no way she'd be able to sleep, even though

dawn was less than an hour away and she was exhausted. Solenne threw herself down onto the sofa and curled up to watch TV, but memories quickly took her over.

Closing her eyes, she listened to the sounds of the night around her. Insects scurried in the grass near her feet, another world so alive co-existing with hers. The deep call of an owl echoed nearby, and she opened her eyes to see its lush feathers of mottled tan and gold and its yellow eyes searching for its mate, but for as long as she watched the beautiful creature, it remained alone on its perch.

Sitting outside at night had become a habit born out of loneliness for her. More and more, Teagan was absent from this house and her life. Other women, other vampires took him away from her, as she feared they would after hearing his words to his brother that night.

And Declan? Each night she yearned to tell him how she dreamed of him—his strong hands caressing her body, his sensual mouth bringing her the exquisite pleasure she knew it could give her—but he remained aloof, seemingly content to watch in dutiful silence as his brother neglected her as he'd promised.

Declan's quiet strength had kept her from going mad on all those nights alone, but she wished for so much more. At times, she even wondered if he avoided her, his brother's cast off.

In truth, Teagan had never promised her forever when he sired her. She'd just hoped for it. The wishes of a young woman in love died hard. But she should have seen the truth of who Teagan was. He never kept it hidden, after all.

She was still his, though. Not interested enough to even return home most nights, he remained the only man she could give herself to by vampire law.

A neglectful sire, but her sire, nonetheless.

If only he'd release her...

Her mind buzzed with treacherous thoughts. No, I must resist what my very soul desires.

She hoped a walk in the night air might clear her mind. Solenne entered the garden pathway outlined with tall hedges and struggled to clear her mind of what she knew would only bring harm to those she loved. Footsteps shook her from her thoughts, and she turned to see Declan behind her.

"Teagan called. He's not coming back for a while. Something to do with Vasilije."

Solenne smiled at his lie. "I understand."

"Has he agreed to let you sire?" His voice verged on pity.

Shaking her head, she smiled at the question, if not the sound of pity in his tone. She'd never even considered siring another vampire. "No, but I've never asked."

"Don't make excuses for him," Declan said angrily. "He doesn't deserve it."

"I'll be fine. I have everything I need—a beautiful home, Teagan's money, and more freedom than most of us can dream of."

Declan's expression clouded over. "Freedom can be just as much a prison. Trust me. I know."

"Is that why you stayed here? I know it's not for your brother."

He grimaced as if in pain and looked away from her.

"I'm sorry things between you haven't worked out."

She understood his disappointment. He'd also hoped for something that never could be.

Stepping closer, he stood in front of her and looked at her with a look she'd never seen from him before. It reminded her of how Teagan had looked at her in those first wonderful days of her life as a vampire.

"I stayed here because of you, Solenne."

"Me?"

"You."

Before she could respond, he kissed her, and everything began to swim around her. Everything she'd fantasized about how his lips would feel on hers paled in comparison to the delicious sensations his kiss produced in her. Forceful, yet yielding, his mouth crushed against hers. Soft, full lips feasted on her desire, taking and increasing it at the same time.

The feelings his touch created threatened to overwhelm her. Whimpering into his mouth, she feared both continuing down the path their passions had led them to and stopping, never to have the sweet taste of him on her lips again.

"This is wrong. No matter how much I want you, I'm still his," she said as she finally broke the kiss.

"I don't care. But from this moment on, you're not his. You're mine."

Mine. Did the man who spoke those words so full of love even exist anymore? Was the man she'd given her heart and soul to—Declan—inside him somewhere, or had he been eliminated by the man Saint had become?

A century of missing him pressed on her heart. There had been men in those years, some she even cared for, but no one had ever taken his place. After a while, it had just become easier to be alone than wish that the male next to her was Declan. Often, she'd been sure it was a foolish wish, but that desire to be with him again never went away, no matter how much she tried to convince herself she should just forget him.

Solenne groggily looked around for some indication of the time and saw the clock on the fireplace mantle. 3:38.

Stretching her body, she worked to smooth out the kinks from lying on the sofa all day. Her back arched and her legs felt like they'd been twisted like pretzels for hours. By the time she made it to the kitchen, she was cursing her age.

A noise from the side of the house Saint's room was on made her instantly forget her body's aches and pains, and she raced toward his room, her heart pounding wildly in her chest.

Was he...?

Were they...?

The door was closed, so she opened it just enough to see if what she feared was true. The shutters that kept out the sun were closed, and in the darkness of the room all that could be seen were the outlines of their bodies. Saint lay on his back on the bed and Maria sat on top of him, her arms above her head.

Tears blurred Solenne's vision, but she couldn't look away. Jealousy settled into her chest like a two-ton weight as she saw the truth.

Saint was making love to a vampire.

Maria rocked back from his body, and Solenne watched the woman who'd dashed her hopes clasp her hands together high in the air. She'd won what Solenne had so wished could be hers.

As the tears rolled down her cheeks, Solenne saw the faint outline of an object in Maria's hands that made her eyes widen in terror.

"No!"

In a blur, she was next to the bed, her hands on Maria's wrists. The woman was stronger and no matter how hard Solenne squeezed, the wooden stake continued toward Saint's heart.

Hatred flashed from Maria's eyes. Solenne felt panic like she'd never felt before. "Don't do this! He's your sire. Saint, wake up!"

Her arms began to shake violently as Maria's strength finally overpowered hers. Beneath his vampire, Saint woke as Solenne's arms finally gave out. The stake crashed down toward his body, just missing his heart when he turned out of its way.

Maria leapt from the bed, but Saint was on her in a flash, holding her fast to the wall.

"Why? Why the fuck would you come here to kill me?" he asked in a voice laced with pain.

Maria turned away from him, but he grabbed her face and forced her to look at him. "Why? Tell me what the fuck I ever did to deserve that?"

"What did you do? How have you treated me? All of us. Other vampires are treated with love and respect. You treat us like outcasts, only wanting us when you need to feed. We mean nothing to you."

Saint stared at her and said nothing, but Solenne couldn't let him be attacked so viciously without saying something in his defense. "He created you. Gave you the life you now enjoy. Gave you the freedom to go wherever you please. Without him, who would you be?"

Maria sneered at her words. "I see you have someone who believes there's more to your heart than just empty darkness. Maybe she's felt something more than your coldness."

"You'd kill me for that?"

"When the Archons summoned me to kill you, I let

myself remember a night so long ago. A new vampire, I came to you wanting you, my sire. Do you remember that night, Declan? Do you remember how I kissed you, so full of love and devotion for the one who'd given me a whole new life? I would have given anything for you to be like other sires. Do you remember what you said to me?"

Saint's shoulders hunched slightly, and he lowered his head. "No."

"You said, 'I can give you everything but that.' I didn't want everything! I wanted love from the one who'd created me!"

Maria's words were full of venom, but Saint remained still in the face of her hatred. "Go and tell the Archons I live."

He dropped his hands, releasing her, and stepped back.

"I have a job to do, sire. Wherever you go, no place will be safe. They will not accept failure. For your crimes against our kind, you must die."

Solenne heard a low growl and then something snapped in Saint. In a blur, he grabbed the stake from the bed and jammed it into Maria's chest. An anguished cry escaped from her throat, and then she was dust.

Saint stumbled back into Solenne's arms, and she held him to her. "I should've let her go. She didn't deserve this."

"Don't. She planned to kill you. If you didn't stake her, I would've."

Turning in her arms, he looked down into her eyes and kissed the top of her head. "Now I'm the criminal they claimed I was. She won't be the last. It isn't safe for

you to be near me anymore, Solenne. Whatever you
agreed to with Vasilije, you didn't agree to this."

Solenne shook her head. "I agreed to keep you safe
and that still stands." Walking away toward the door, she
turned and said quietly, "All these years later and I still
can't bear to think of a world without you in it."

12

Solenne watched as the Archon moved between offices judging cases for hours as she filed official papers and listened to Rochelle give a dissertation on the popes of Avignon. He seemed particularly out of sorts, and with each defendant who passed her desk, she was more convinced that any time she'd be forced to spend with him that night would be painful.

As the last vampire was lead away, Rochelle concluded her history lecture and began straightening her desk before she left. For once, Solenne wished she would stay late.

"Lena, please make sure to finish filing all the papers for tonight's cases. I don't want Mr. Verrater to worry about anything after working so hard tonight."

Solenne watched her carefully place three pens one next to the other and move around her desk toward the door. "Rochelle, do you have plans tonight? Would you like to order in and hang out while I finish?"

"Oh, I wish I could, Lena. I have to clean my house to get ready for the painters. They're coming at sundown tomorrow. Have a great night. Remember the filing for Mr. Verrater."

Rochelle happily strolled away, leaving Solenne alone with her work. And Marc Verrater.

It didn't take long to complete the filing, and then she sat at her desk waiting for his summons. Solenne's legs shook as she sat wishing he'd forget she was there. The heels of her shoes made clicking noises as they tapped against the plastic floor protector beneath her desk, only making her more on edge.

Each minute that passed made her more desperate to go home. There Declan waited, needing someone after what had happened with Maria. Solenne wrestled with the idea of just leaving—just going to the man she loved to take care of him instead of spending another night hoping she'd learn something in passing as the Archon spoke. But she couldn't leave. What if tonight was the night that he let slip some fragment of information that could help Declan and the rest of the Sons defeat these bastards?

By 3:15, she wondered if she'd been spared her time with Verrater. She'd sat at her desk for almost two hours without hearing a noise from his office. Cautiously, she let herself relax, lowering her shoulders to ease her aching back wracked with tension. A deep breath and then another and she closed her eyes, relaxed at last and hopeful she'd be home safe and sound with Declan soon.

"Lena, come in."

Opening her eyes, she saw him standing in the

doorway of his office. His black dress shirt remained buttoned at the collar, and he still wore an expensive silk tie as he did each night.

But as in the past, that would change.

"Yes, sir."

Dread filled her, making the short walk from her desk to his office difficult as her legs felt like they were weighted down with lead. He stood leaning against the doorframe, his deep blue eyes watching her every move toward him.

This was his ritual every time he took her. She wouldn't be spared this night.

As she reached him, she stopped and turned to face him. Her part in this was to let him do as he willed, and even as every cell in her body cried out for her to flee from this place and him, she played her role perfectly, knowing that her welfare was dwarfed by the need for all of her kind to do whatever they could to defeat Verrater and his fellow Archons.

His face was the picture of cold sensuality. The desire was there, but the feeling was lacking. He stared down at her and his dark gaze traveled not to the lips he'd kiss or the breasts he'd fondle but to the spot where her neck met her shoulder, the very spot he'd sink his fangs into, piercing her vein and taking her blood.

Desired for that precious liquid, she was also forced to give him whatever else he desired if she expected to keep up her charade. By the look in his eyes, Solenne saw that he wouldn't be satisfied with just her blood tonight.

"Go to the anteroom. Be undressed when I join you."

Solenne made her way through his office to a smaller

room and began to undress as ordered. As she lay her clothes over a rack near the door, careful to make sure they didn't wrinkle and show signs of what she was about to do, she thought of questions she could ask about the order of death against Declan, Rochelle's boring trivia of Avignon, anything to keep her mind off what would happen in just minutes.

Naked, she stood beside the sofa and waited for him to come. He kept the room hotter than the rest of his chambers, but she still stood shaking, her ears trained on the sound of his footsteps across the marble floor.

How long she waited she couldn't tell. It seemed like forever and mere minutes at the same time. When he finally arrived, she had convinced herself once again that no matter what he required, she'd acquiesce knowing this was what she had to do.

He stood in front of her, and she began her part in their terrible play by loosening the tie from his neck. Carefully, she unknotted the silk and slid it from under his collar. He took it from her hand and draped it over the back of the sofa.

"You look lovely, Lena."

His compliment fell on deaf ears, meaningless to her. Solenne's fingers shook as she unbuttoned his shirt, her knuckles vibrating against his Adam's apple as he moaned his pleasure at her touch. Each button undone revealed more of his well-defined chest and stomach, and even as Solenne wished to look away she couldn't avoid the power his body exuded.

Shame flooded over her at the mere thought that the Archon or any part of him could appeal to her. Never once before had she felt anything but revulsion at his presence. Even now, his touch made her cringe and she clung to that sensation as he kissed her, his lips pressing hard against hers demanding her submission.

His hands slid down her sides, and came to rest on her ass, making her shiver as goose bumps erupted on her skin. Squeezing, his hands pulled her toward his body, and she felt his erection press against her near her hip.

"Tonight, we have cause for celebration, dear Lena," he whispered near her ear. His breath hit her skin, and the vicious click of his fangs snapping into place filled her ears.

"Sir?" she asked, struggling to control the trembling in her voice as the fear of him was replaced by a feeling of dread at the thought that as she'd passively sat out at her desk, he'd succeeded in killing Declan.

"I move up in the ranks of the Archons. My time here in France nears its completion once the end of Declan Collins is complete."

Verrater's fangs grazed her skin as he prepared to feed from her, but she pressed for more information, knowing she risked his wrath but not caring. This is what she'd sacrificed so much for, and she would see this through to the end.

"He's been eliminated then?"

His lips moved left and right against her neck as he shook his head. "Not yet, but I have all assurances of success. Now, no more talk, Lena."

The Archon plunged his fangs into her neck as he pressed his fingertips painfully into her shoulders. The combination of his bite and his hold on her should have been too much to bear, but Solenne's mind raced with thoughts. Had Maria told him where Declan was, or had she acted before informing him? Did he believe she'd already succeeded tonight? Or did he know what had happened and was sending another to kill Declan as she stood there forced to let him feed from her? Emily had obviously never met Declan and hadn't been intended as the assassin, so had he simply used her to feel out her own loyalty to him? And what did he mean he was moving up in the ranks and his time in France was near completion? Where was he going?

Solenne felt him pull away from her neck, and she readied herself for what was to come next. He lifted his head and facing her, licked his lips to catch the remaining few drops of blood that had trickled out to the corner of his mouth.

"You are a rare gift, dear Lena," he said as he motioned toward the sofa. She sat and he stood looking down at her as he stepped out of his pants to stand naked in front of her. "A rare gift indeed."

From the other room a voice yelled, "Archon? Are you here?"

Solenne saw the anger cross Verrater's face and leaned back instinctively, expecting his rage to explode around her. Instead, his look changed to one of interest and he quickly dressed.

As he turned to join the stranger in the next room, he smiled. "Next time, dear, we'll pick up where we left off."

Happy for the reprieve, Solenne began to dress and wondered who the man was who held such sway over the Archon. His voice was unfamiliar, and it didn't sound like that of anyone of any real importance like many of the vampires she'd encountered in Verrater's office.

Hoping to see who it was, she finished dressing and hurried out into the other room, but there was no sign of either man.

VASILIJE RELAXED as Terek and Dante talked quietly on the other side of the room. Out of all the Sons, they appeared least affected by the utter lack of progress the group had achieved since gathering in Romania. Terek had taken to the task of guiding the young vampire who was so gifted yet so reckless, but as of yet if he'd had any success in making him more than a clyten, Vasilije hadn't seen it.

"You look a million miles away."

Next to him, Sasa stood with that warm smile that had the power to melt his heart every time he saw it. "No, just a lot on my mind, love."

Taking a seat next to him, she sat quietly for a long time. Vasilije felt calm with her and appreciated just having Sasa near, even in silence.

"Vasilije, have we heard anything from Solenne? I'm worried you all expect too much from her to deal with Saint. He doesn't even like vampire females."

"She's tough, Sasa. She came to us offering her help. Solenne knows how to handle herself and Saint."

To be honest, he wasn't at all sure any woman could handle Saint, least of all Solenne. She was tough, no doubt. But Saint's reaction to her when he'd first realized she was the one vampire willing to help him wasn't promising. And the fact that he still refused her blood was another problem. Without vampire blood, he'd weaken and be vulnerable to attack, which could come at any time.

Sasa squeezed his hand. "I sensed her fear when she first arrived the other night. It was as clear as day. Why would she be afraid of someone you claim was an old friend of hers?"

"Are you sure it was fear you felt?"

Nodding, she said, "I'm sure of it. I know I've had to get used to having my empath ability with being a vampire, but her emotions were so strong when she arrived here, I couldn't help but be affected by them. She was afraid, Vasilije, and now she's stuck in that house with him."

Vasilije questioned why she'd have volunteered to hide Saint in her own house if she feared him. Saint was no doubt difficult, but that had never manifested itself in harming women. He didn't doubt Sasa's empath power, but was there something he and the other Sons were missing about Solenne—something that could be deadly to one of their own?

As he tried to piece together the puzzle of Saint and Solenne, Arnie arrived for a meeting he'd requested. A valuable spy for the group, he was odd, to say the least. By all accounts, he was quite old for a vampire, but he seemed stuck in the 1970s, of all decades.

"Vasilije, what's shakin'?"

Turning to Sasa, Vasilije whispered, "Make sure everyone is out of sight until he leaves."

As Sasa closed the door to his office, leaving the two men alone, Vasilije smiled and offered him a seat.

"Thanks, man. My dogs are barkin' tonight."

Arnie sat down across from where Vasilije sat and began tapping his knuckles on the arm of the chair. He made Vasilije somewhat uncomfortable—more edgy than anything else—when he was near. Vasilije had never asked Sasa about her sense of him, but he'd noticed how she seemed to pay very close attention whenever he met with them.

Sasa returned and Arnie began his report. "I have something very interesting. Seems those fuckers are using vampires familiar with the targets instead of hunters. That bitch Tatiana wasn't just some angry woman from your past."

Turning toward Sasa, Arnie raised his hand and apologized. "Sorry about my language."

"No need. Consider me no different than Vasilije."

"Thanks. Using friends and former lovers seems like a nice personal touch to killing someone, don't you think?"

"Do we have any idea who got the nod with Saint?" Vasilije asked as he thought about the Archons' choice of Tatiana as his assassin.

Arnie shook his head. "Not yet, but he's a tough one."

"Why?"

"Because he's had so little contact with his vampires for so long, the Archons are having a hard time locating possible assassins."

"Solenne found out they're portraying him as a sexual deviant who mistreated his vampires," Vasilije said, still not believing this entirely.

"I don't doubt it. They'll do whatever they can to make him Public Enemy Number One."

"It just seems odd that they'd not use who he really is to do that."

Arnie began tapping his knuckles on the arm of the chair again. "Well, I don't know what those bastards are thinking, but I'd put money on Solenne. She's in this body and soul."

Vasilije felt instantly uneasy about his description of Solenne and thought his choice of words odd. Body and soul?

Arnie stood up and straightened his long shirt that hung far below his waist. "I'm out, but I'm keeping my finger on the pulse of the bad guys. I'll let you know when I find something out."

"Thanks for everything, Arnie," Vasilije said as he escorted him to the door.

TEN MINUTES LATER, the rest of the Sons sat around Vasilije's office. Turning to Sion, Vasilije saw concern in his expression. "Your face says you have something on your mind."

"How much do we know about who we have spying for us?"

"Solenne was one of Teagan's. I've known her since he turned her. And Arnie, I've known for years. Damian, I don't know at all, but he comes from the Order."

"Let's assume for the moment that Damian is okay since he came recommended from the Order. What about this Arnie guy?"

Vasilije turned to Sasa. "Did you have any sense of him, now or at any other time?"

"He's anxious whenever he's here. That's all I ever get from him."

"He says the Archons are having a hard time choosing someone to do the job with Saint."

"Because there are so many who would agree to do it?" Dante asked.

Vasilije and Terek both shot Dante a look telling him now was not the time for his bullshit with Saint. Silently chastised, he put up his hands as if to say he was sorry and sat back in his chair.

"No. Because he's not close enough to any of them. They don't know where to find him, thankfully. But remember, Solenne said they were going with the sex fiend angle."

Sion folded his arms across his chest. "That hasn't sat right with me since Solenne told us. It makes no sense. Saint's already an outcast to many vampires because he sleeps with human women exclusively. Why make him seem something else when there's already a good enough reason some would like to see him gone? Something's not right."

"Are you saying you have doubts about Solenne?" Terek asked.

"I don't think Sion was saying that. I think he was just expressing what some of us have been thinking," Vasilije said quickly.

"I think we need to be careful. This Arnie guy gives me a bad feeling. And I'm not sure about Solenne either," Sion answered.

"They're all we have at the moment, Sion," Terek said. "And so far, I get nothing odd from Solenne, but I admit I haven't intentionally tried to listen to her thoughts. And as for Arnie, I'll heed Sasa's impression that he simply seems to be a nervous creature."

"Vampires, people, whatever are nervous for a reason, Terek. From now on, I think you should see if you can somehow spend some time in his head to give us an idea what's really on Arnie's mind," Sion warned. "And as for Solenne, the jury's still out for me on her."

13

Two hours in Solenne's gym couldn't push the thought of her from Saint's mind. Tonight she was at the Archon's, putting herself in danger to keep him safe as he spent his time in the French countryside. She never spoke of what she was forced to endure there, but he'd noticed her wincing in pain more than once after her visits to that fucking place.

The thought of her hurt at the hands of one of them made him blind with rage. Again and again, he pummeled the bag until every muscle in his body ached, but still his rage remained unabated.

Saint fixed his eyes on the clock. 4:12. *She should be back by now.*

He'd give her ten minutes more and then do what he should have done the first time he watched her go to that place.

.   .   .

SOLENNE SAT with her head in her hands at the kitchen table, her bruised arms the evidence of her sacrifice. Saint lightly ran his finger over the purple mark where he suspected the Archon had brutally misused her and cringed in anger at the look of pain he saw in her eyes when she looked up at him.

A growl escaped from his lips and his fangs slammed down into his mouth. "Who did this?"

Pushing past him, she shook her head. "Don't. If this is what I have to endure to keep you safe and help the Sons defeat those bastards, then I do it willingly."

"Tell me who did this, Solenne. I owe him."

She spun around to face him, and the pained sound in her voice made him hate himself. "Why? So you can make everything I've done meaningless? So you can get yourself killed?"

Before he could answer, she was gone, but he'd seen the tears in her eyes. Anger mixed with the need to protect her, churning his gut into knots until he had to see her.

He had to let her know what she'd done wasn't meaningless.

Her door was open, and she stood with her back to him. Already out of her clothes, she wore only a tank top and boy shorts that clung to every perfect curve on her body. His cock stiffened as his eyes took in the sight of her gorgeous legs. Long and lean, they were the kind of legs a man loved wrapped around him as he slid in and out of her wet cunt.

"Solenne," he said almost in a whisper to not startle her, but it didn't work. She spun around with her arms covering her full breasts that strained against the thin fabric of her tank top, but she couldn't cover the bruises along her collarbone and across her shoulders.

Obviously inflicted that night, their redness had begun to fade to a deep purple where fingers had pressed roughly into her tender skin. Solenne saw the look of shock he didn't try to hide from his eyes and scrambled to grab a shirt from the back of a nearby chair.

"What is this?"

"Nothing. Just leave it be."

Saint took the shirt from her hand and threw it on the bed. "No." Dipping his head, he softly pressed his lips to the darkest bruise on her left shoulder. *Fucking Archon!*

Gingerly, he ran his fingers over her skin, gently touching each bruise before raising his head to look at her. "Solenne, I promise you here and now I'm going to kill the one who did this. I'll drain him drop by drop until he begs for the release a stake will bring."

Eyes wide with tears looked up at him, their blue color pale and watery. "Saint, don't touch me like this if you don't mean it."

He meant it. He'd meant it in every dream he'd had of finally returning to her. Taking her face in his hands, he kissed her long and deep, drinking in the delicious taste of the lips he'd missed for so long.

God, he'd yearned to once again feel the touch of her skin next to his! Year upon year of lonely nights interrupted only by pale replacements ebbed from his memory now as his hands once again learned of the woman he'd always loved.

Solenne molded to him, setting his senses ablaze. His body craved to join with her, to finally reclaim that piece of his heart lost so painfully nearly a century ago. He slid his hands under her shirt to her breasts and worshipped them—their fullness in his palms, their deep pink tips pebbled from desire that begged for his mouth's attention.

"Come."

Taking her hand, he led her to the shower. "Don't move." A quick twist of the faucet handle and warm water streamed down from the showerhead.

"Do I look like I need a shower?" she asked in a teasing tone as he slipped the tank top over her head.

Saint looked down at her sexy mouth as he slid his thumbs under the waist of her shorts. "Always fighting me."

Crouching in front of her, he slid the shorts down her legs and off her feet. Eye level with her pussy, he looked up and licked his lips. "I hope you don't plan on fighting me now."

He didn't wait for a reply before he drew his finger up her wet slit. Solenne's eyebrows knitted and she bit her lip. Her eyes slowly closed and tiny moans filled his ears.

"Don't close your eyes. Watch me."

Solenne obeyed and her eyes grew wide as he slid his thumbs through her delicate folds to open her up, unveiling to his eager eyes her excited clit. Saint inched closer to her soft skin and whispered against her, "I've waited so long for this."

Softly musky, her taste danced on his tongue, thrilling him. He ran his tongue over her clit, eliciting a groan that traveled straight to his cock pushing against his pants. So responsive, she showed her pleasure at every lap against her skin.

"Yes...there. Right there," she cooed.

Her moans grew louder as her climax edged closer. Saint slid inside her slick channel and massaged that spot deep inside her with a fingertip. Her body reacted just as he knew it would, greedily closing around his finger. So close, she tilted her hips to bring him deeper into her.

"Declan, don't stop. God, don't stop!"

Solenne's voice trailed off, and Saint felt her orgasm take her over. Taking her swollen nub between his lips, he sucked as she whimpered sounds of perfect pleasure.

Finally, when her body had finished its ecstasy, she cried, "My legs are going to give out, Declan!"

Saint grabbed the backs of her thighs as her legs buckled underneath her. It had been so long since he'd had the joy of reveling in the feeling of pleasing one of his kind. God, he'd missed this!

He stood and smiled, ready for round two. Steam hung above their heads, and Solenne pulled at his clothes to undress him.

"I hope there's some hot water left," she said with a smile as he stepped out of his pants. As she stroked his already hard cock, she licked her lips and added, "I'd hate to have this ruined by cold water."

Nuzzling her neck, he murmured against her moist skin, "It could be ice water. Doesn't matter."

Saint led her into the glass shower and closed the door behind them. When he turned back to face her, he stopped short, struck by how beautiful she was as she stood there soaking wet in front of him.

Pulling her to him, he pressed his body to hers and kissed her deeply. She arched into him, tilted her head back, and smiled that same sexy grin that had seduced him so many times before. Smoothing the wet hair from her face, he stared into her beautiful eyes, letting himself get lost in them.

"God, you're gorgeous," he said as he slid his hands to cradle her face. "Every day since the last time I felt your body next to mine this is the face that's filled my dreams."

"Don't talk about that, please. It hurts too much to even think of it. All those years lost."

Solenne closed her eyes and lowered her head. "I'm so sorry, Declan. I never wanted to lose you."

He shook his head and kissed her forehead. "Don't. There's nothing back there for us now. Everything we feel is here now and every night from this moment on."

Leaning in, he brushed his lips across hers and pulled back to gaze into those eyes so full of everything he'd ever wanted in this world.

Sexy, strong Solenne.

His body begged to feel hers next to him, around him, and his muscles ached from the tension of denying himself for so long. Finally, after years of being without the love of one of his kind, he'd returned home to the only vampire he'd ever shared himself with.

DECLAN LIFTED HER, easing her back against the wet tile, and Solenne held on to this neck as she wrapped her legs around him. His body, every inch muscular and hard, felt strong and powerful next to hers. The abs she'd fantasized touching days earlier pressed hard against her, making her pussy run wet in anticipation.

He kissed her neck and she felt the sharp tips of his fangs scrape lightly over her skin as he whispered in a strained voice, "I need to feel you around my cock when I taste you."

"Yes...God, yes," she moaned as she tilted her hips forward to take him inside her.

Slowly, he pressed into her body, his thickness pushing against her walls forcing her to take all of him. Every inch closer made her more desperate to feel him buried completely inside her.

Her fingernails dug into his neck as her eyes urged him to give her all of him. Declan stared at her and something wild in his eyes made her unable to break the connection. It was as if he were seeing her for the first time.

Finally, as their bodies met, he groaned her name and buried his fangs in her neck. He was primal, thrusting into her body as he sucked what he needed from her. Every pull on her vein sent a ribbon of need through her body straight to her cunt, and with each thrust into her, he eased that need only to make it spike again.

His hands on her back bore the brunt of his pounding into her, shielding her from crashing into the wall each time his cock entered her. Over and over, he stroked in and out of her, touching some spot lost to her for so long she'd forgotten the true pleasure her body could experience.

Things began to spin around her as he stayed at her neck, but she couldn't deny him what he needed. She knew she should cry out to stop him, but she didn't, knowing the risk and not caring. She'd taken this away from him then. She'd give him this now.

Declan raised his head and stilled his thrusting into her, his dark eyes wilder than before. His mouth hung open slightly, and from his fangs her blood dripped down his chin. Panting, he ran his tongue over his lips and growled as it caught her blood.

He looked different than she'd ever seen him. Sensual and animalistic. For a moment, she stiffened in fear. The Declan she'd known had never been like this. Yes, he'd known how to please her body in ways no other man ever had, but never before had she'd seen no trace of tenderness in his face like she did now.

As she watched him, part frightened and part enthralled at how sensual he'd become, he wiped his chin with the back of his hand and licked his lips.

"You taste so fucking good."

"Declan..."

"I can feel you racing through my veins. It feels better than anything I've ever felt. It's like every time I've ever pushed my body to the point of exhaustion—that point right before when my body feels more alive than I ever thought it could."

As he spoke, his eyes traveled to the spot on her neck where he'd taken from her.

"Declan, I'm feeling a little weak."

"Take from me all you need," he said as he leaned in to kiss her.

The feel of his hard, muscular neck against her lips made whatever fear she'd harbored melt away. Declan moved a hand to the back of her head and held her fast to him, demanding she take from him as he had from her.

Her fangs pressed into his skin and as she savored the first taste of him on her tongue, he thrust his hips forward, filling her completely once again. His other hand on the small of her back pulled her into him, and he began pumping into her as she took his blood into her body.

He tasted so exotic and foreign, like nothing she'd ever experienced before, but somewhere in there was the familiar. The combination made her body come alive, and she craved the release he could give her.

"I need..."

Her brain couldn't seem to tell her mouth what words to say. She needed so much. To come with him deep inside her. To feel him come inside her. To never lose him again. To feel this every night for the rest of her life.

She hoped her eyes would do the pleading her mouth couldn't. Staring into his wild eyes, she saw he understood.

In a voice that touched the spot his cock had so expertly found, he said, "I know, baby. Let me give you what you need."

He took her hands from his neck and pressed them against the wall above her head. Weaving his fingers in between hers, he pushed her arms high as he pumped into her body. He held her under his control, but she wouldn't have fought him for anything in the world. His powerful body crashed against her softer body, but she didn't care. Every thrust of his cock inched her closer to the release her body begged for.

Her arms ached, the pain radiating from the pressure of his hands on hers and her wrists against the wall. It didn't matter. Her legs throbbed as they held him to her desperately, rubbing against his flexing back muscles, but it didn't matter.

Declan pressed his forehead to hers and panted warm

breath in her face. "Come for me. Give yourself to me again," he groaned.

Turning her head, she bared her neck. She needed to feel him take from her as she came again, the joining of her body with his in the most intimate way of her kind. "Take from me."

Pumping even faster into her now, he let his mouth hover over where she desperately yearned to feel him again. "Declan, don't make me beg!"

She heard him say, "Never, baby," and then he latched onto her neck, his teeth burying into her skin and the vein beneath.

Her orgasm rolled over her like a freight rain, taking her breath away. Her legs squeezed his waist tightly as her cunt spasmed against his thick cock, milking him to his own release. His groans into her body echoed in the shower and then he exploded into her, coating her channel in hot liquid.

Declan lapped closed the holes he'd made in her skin but remained at her neck as his body released torrents into hers. Solenne felt him kiss her softly as he stilled against her. Something cold sprayed on her and she realized the water falling onto his back was like ice.

"You must be freezing. Let's get out of here."

Silently, he shook his head and released her hands. Cradling his face, she lifted him from her neck and saw the remnants of his feeding from her again staining his lips a deep red. Still wild looking, he opened his eyes and something of the soul she'd known all those years ago shone in them.

"Declan?"

When he spoke, his words sounded like they were

being torn from him. "I can't live without this anymore. I can't live without you anymore. I don't care about the Archons, my part in the Sons, or anything else. As long as I have you, none of that matters."

"Don't say that. It does matter."

"No, it doesn't. I spent a century alone, an outcast from the world, but what was worse was not having you. I won't live like that again."

Solenne ran her hands over his closely shaved head and kissed the mouth that had just said the words she'd prayed to hear since the day she'd lost him. "I'm sorry we lost all those years. I can't bear the idea of losing you now to the Archons."

Declan gently traced his finger over her collarbone. "I intend on making up for lost time, and the Archons don't know what they're up against. I was going to be hard to kill before. Now that I have something to live for and someone to kill for, they're the ones that need to worry."

14

Saint stretched his legs and felt the ache in them ebb from his muscles. Tired after getting just a few hours rest, he nonetheless wouldn't have traded his exhaustion for anything in the world. Memories of the previous night with Solenne danced through his mind, and his cock hardened at the thought of making love to her again.

Her body still pressed against his, her breasts rubbing against his ribs as they rose and fell with each breath. He threaded his fingers through her hair and enjoyed the silky feel of it against his skin.

Solenne turned and looked up at him. "Sleep well?"

"I don't think three hours of sleep adds up to well," he said with a chuckle.

Tracing her finger over his nipple, she smiled up at him. "I should have let you sleep."

"You're right where you belong," he said as he wrapped his legs around her and settled her body between them.

Shyly, she slid up his body and kissed him on the lips. "I could stay here for the rest of time."

So could he. Forget the rest of the world—Archons who wanted him dead, vampires who cared more about who he fucked than who he was, prophecies, Sons, and the Order. All he needed was right there in bed with him, where she ought to be.

"But I have to go out tonight."

He heard the fear in her voice and knew what she meant. She had to go to the Archon's. Fuck, he hated the thought of her anywhere near him!

Saint lifted her chin to see her face. "I want you to know I meant what I said last night."

"Declan, I..."

"Don't think about it. Just know he will know what hatred feels like before I end his life."

Saint held her close to him, needing to feel the love of the woman who lay in his arms. This time he'd make sure things were different. This time nothing was going to take her from him.

He rolled her over onto her back and hovered over her, his weight resting on his forearms. She looked up at him with those watery blue eyes filled with fear at what she had to do once she left their bed that night, and it tore at his gut.

He was supposed to protect her. Not the other way around.

Gently, he lowered himself and entered her, needing to prove to her he could take care of what she needed. Her body welcomed his invasion, taking him completely. She clung to him, her hands clutching at his neck as he thrust in long, slow strokes into her slickness.

His teeth cut into his lower lip as the need to taste her blood surged in him. The desire intensified with every plunge into her, but he knew he shouldn't. She'd almost let him go too far when he'd taken from her the first time.

But he needed it.

She was like his drug.

He pressed his nose to her neck and inhaled the sweet smell of her as he felt her pulse quicken. Its steady beat pounded against his lips taunting him. His body telegraphed his need with shorter, faster stabs into her body as it began to overtake his senses.

"Solenne, I need to taste you on my tongue, but I don't know if I can control what's inside me that wants more."

He let her roll him onto his back and watched as she straddled him, his cock still deep inside her. More beautiful than any other woman he'd ever met, she personified strength and power as she pushed her hands onto his shoulders and began to slowly fuck him.

"Take what you need, Declan. I know you'd never hurt me."

He'd sooner die than hurt her now.

He pulled her down on him, holding her tightly against his body as he found the tender spot just below her ear. Silently, he hoped he'd be able to stop and sunk his fangs into her, puncturing her vein that instantly flooded his mouth with her precious fluid.

Her blood made his head spin and his heart pound in his ears, almost drowning out the sounds of her moans. His hips pushed up from the bed, ramming his cock into her slick pussy.

Solenne pulled his head to her neck and held him there, letting him know she trusted him. Each gulp of her blood made him stronger, and he fought the demon inside that craved more, no matter what the cost to the woman in his arms.

Tearing his mouth from her neck, he struggled for control as she continued to ride him to climax. She felt so good, her tight cunt wrapped around his cock, squeezing him until he craved release, and to take her blood as he came inside her would be heaven.

"You look so sexy with my blood on your lips," she said sweetly as she rocked back and forth on him.

With his thumb, he touched her swollen clit and she bucked wildly. "And you look so sexy riding my cock."

Solenne ran her tongue over her fangs and smacked her lips as he rubbed tiny circles over her nub. "I'm thirsty," she whispered in a needy voice.

"Take from me. Everything I am is yours."

The feel of her mouth taking what she needed to exist sent his body into overdrive. He thrust into her willing body one last time before his release exploded into her, and a sense of complete happiness took him over.

This is what life was meant to be. The love of a good woman in his heart and in his bed. The feel of bringing one of his kind the pleasure he'd only given human women more nights than he could count.

Solenne stilled on top of him and murmured softly in his ear the words he'd missed for so long. "I love you. I always have from the moment I saw the true soul behind those dark eyes."

She slid her tongue like a whisper over his neck and rose to kiss his lips. Her face was flushed with satisfaction, and the pleasure of knowing he'd given her what she needed made his heart swell with love.

"My Solenne. My life was empty without you. No love, no meaning. Nothing. There has been no one in my heart since the last time I pledged my life to you."

He wiped the tears that ran down her cheek before she lifted his hand to cover her heart. "This is yours, Declan. It always has been. It's waited for you to return."

Saint felt her heart beat beneath his palm as she placed her hand on his. For the first time in a century, he wasn't alone.

Sliding from the bed, she began to ready herself for her time at the Archon's. Saint moved to stand behind her and brought her close to his body, not wanting to let her go, but he knew she had to, at least for tonight. Following her to the main hallway, he began to miss her already.

"I'll be back before dawn. Maybe you should try to get some rest because I think a repeat of last night is in order," Solenne said as she wrapped her arms around his neck. "You better be careful. I might be too much for you."

"You think so? We'll see. But I want you to be careful tonight. In fact, I plan on telling Vasilije we need to find someone else. You can help us better right here with me."

Solenne lifted herself up on her toes and kissed his lips. "You won't get any fight from me. Every time I have to go to Verrater's I hate it. But there might not be anyone else who can get in there like I have."

Saint kissed her deeply, his tongue playing with hers as his desire began to rise once again. Pressed against him, her body ignited the urge to sweep her into his arms and carry her back to his bed.

Knowing she had to go, he reluctantly broke the kiss and pressed his forehead to hers. "The Romanian is a resourceful vampire. Let him figure out who can replace you."

From behind them, Vasilije said, "Thanks, Saint. I think that might be the only nice thing you've ever said about me."

Saint tensed at the sound of the Romanian's voice, but he saw the pleading look in Solenne's eyes not to take his bait and knew she was right. His brother's sire wasn't worth it.

Turning to face him, he held her hand. "Was the door open, Vasilije?"

"Not exactly, and I do apologize to Solenne for intruding. But when you find out why I'm here, you'll understand."

"Since you're smiling, can I assume you've heard when the Archons plan to kill me?"

"Declan," Solenne chastised and playfully grimaced at him.

"Declan? Interesting. No, we don't know when the attack will occur. Hopefully, Solenne, you'll find out something soon."

"About that. We need to find someone else. It's too dangerous for her," Saint said in a voice he reserved only for Vasilije.

"Fine. But about why I'm here."

"Vasilije, you look..." Solenne stopped and took a step back. "How?"

Saint followed her gaze to a figure standing behind Vasilije. For a second, he looked like any other stranger, but quickly Saint recognized the familiar angles of his face.

What stood facing him was a ghost. It had to be.

Solenne stammered a few words he didn't understand and dropped his hand to move closer to Vasilije. "What is this? Vasilije, what's going on?"

The emotion in her voice cut like a knife through Saint's heart. He stepped forward to stand with Solenne, but as he wrapped his arm around her, she slipped out of his hold.

"Teagan! How can this be?" she cried as she threw her arms around his neck. "They said you were dead. I felt you leave this world. How?"

"That's the magic of New Orleans voodoo, love. I'm anything but dead."

Saint's gaze met Vasilije's and he saw the smirk grow on his face. Fucking Romanian!

"Incredible, wouldn't you say, Saint?"

Incredible wasn't the word he'd use to describe his brother rising from the dead. Impossible seemed more appropriate.

Saint heard Teagan ask, "No welcome for your long-lost brother?" and he looked over to see him with his arm around Solenne, who seemed at home next to him after all their years apart. The closeness between them made Saint's stomach knot, and everything he and Solenne had just shared seemed to evaporate before his eyes.

"I'm happy to see you still among the living, Teagan."

His brother—the only family he had left in this world —stood in front of him after nearly one hundred years, and Saint felt the pressure to finally put the past behind him. Solenne's eyes pleaded for him to accept Teagan as she had, and even though jealousy threatened to explode out of him, Saint adored her too much to disappoint her.

"Voodoo trumps the stake then, brother?"

Teagan let out a full laugh and wrapped his arms around him. "You'd be surprised at what that voodoo can do, but no, it can't trump the stake."

"Then what happened? Sasa said that Tatiana woman staked you in front of her right in your house in New Orleans," Solenne said.

Releasing Saint, Teagan backed away and began to explain. "Unfortunately for my friend Jake, Sasa saw him turned to dust that night. Poor guy. He was waiting for me, but that bitch got to him first. I got there to find what she'd done to him and got out quick as I could."

"But I felt you leave this world."

Teagan smiled at Solenne's words. "That's the voodoo. I knew I had to lay low and make Vasilije believe I'd bit it, or I'd be in danger, so I quickly worked a little voodoo I'd learned when I first moved to New Orleans. Wild stuff. I guess it worked pretty well, if the look on your face is any indication."

"Whatever you did, it's good to know I didn't lose another one of my favorites," Vasilije said.

Saint felt like an intruder among them. They were all connected, more it seemed than he was to his own flesh and blood. Sire who'd begat a vampire turned sire who'd begat the woman he loved.

And he was a mere brother, something history had shown Teagan harbored little respect for.

Solenne touched his hand, and he looked down to see where hers joined with his. In his ear, she whispered, "I love you. Thank you for being the bigger man."

Saint looked into her eyes and saw what had been there when she'd been in his arms earlier. "I didn't do it because I'm the bigger man. I did it for you."

"Then I love you even more," she said as she squeezed his hand and stared lovingly into his eyes.

"What are you two whispering about?" Teagan asked, breaking the moment.

"Will you be staying at your sire's house in Romania?" Saint asked before anyone else could answer his brother's question.

Solenne squeezed his hand again and both Vasilije and Teagan appeared confused by his question.

"I'm sure Teagan would like to spend some time with his vampire. And his brother, of course. And you certainly have enough room here, don't you, Solenne?"

Vasilije's phony concern for Teagan's relationship with Solenne made Saint's blood boil. Stroking the back of his hand, she tried to calm him, and Saint remained silent for the moment.

"Of course we do. Declan and I would love to have you stay with us, Teagan."

"It'll be like the old days. Remember our times together, just the three of us?"

Teagan's reminder of the past that linked all of them only served to make Saint uneasy. Every bit as much an intrusive sire as his own, Teagan seemed to have decided to truly reconnect with Solenne. It was his prerogative as her sire, of course, but that didn't make the thought any more welcome in Saint's mind.

"I'll leave you to get reacquainted. Teagan, enjoy yourself, but I want us to talk soon."

Vasilije flashed a satisfied grin and before Saint could remind him about finding a replacement spy for Solenne, he vanished, leaving the three former friends alone.

Together.

Saint watched as Teagan made himself at home, laughing with Solenne about some long-forgotten memory and subtly reminding her of her responsibility as his vampire. But no matter how many times he tried to accept it, Saint couldn't.

He was happy his brother wasn't dead. He wasn't happy he was here with them.

His memories of their past together gnawed at him. For him, very few contained anything worth laughing about.

But at least the Romanian was gone.

Padding up behind Solenne, he placed his hand securely on her shoulder as she listened to Teagan explain the voodoo spell he'd used to avoid suffering the same fate as his friend.

"You should see New Orleans, Solenne. It's like nowhere else in the world. I can't wait to get back. If you'd like, I can show you the town."

"Solenne has to go now."

Teagan's brown eyes grew wide and he raised his eyebrows. "Don't worry, Declan. You'd be welcome to come too."

"Thanks. Excuse us for a minute. Go into the kitchen and help yourself to something to eat. I'll be in to join you in a minute."

Saint led Solenne toward the front door, as Teagan headed for the kitchen. Pulling her into an alcove, he held her to him and kissed her possessively.

"What was that for?" she asked sweetly when he lifted his head to look at her.

"Just a little reminder of last night."

He knew he was acting like a jealous ass, but he didn't

care. Solenne was his and the fact that his long-lost brother returned from the dead was her sire wasn't going to change that.

"Keep those lips ready for when I return from Verrater's. I'm going to want some more reminding."

Solenne stood on her toes and placed a kiss on the tip of his nose. "And don't forget I love you."

Saint ran his fingers along the length of her hair and fondled the ends. Just hearing those sweet words coming out of her beautiful mouth made his heart pound faster. God, the effect she had on him!

"And I intend on reminding you why when you get back. Just be careful. Do you understand. You don't need to get any deep dark secrets from that bastard tonight."

Her smile seemed forced, and he fought the urge to press her on exactly what went on each time she went to the Archon's office, knowing that if she confirmed the suspicions he held in his mind, he wouldn't let the Archon see another night alive.

"I love you, Declan, darkness and all." Looking past him, she added, "Don't let him get to you."

"Don't worry about Lazarus in there. I wouldn't trade my second chance for his for anything in this world."

15

Ramiel and Thane sat quietly at the table that had become their home since arriving at the monastery. Old volumes of Greek and vampire history surrounded them, giving off a musty odor that hung heavy in the cool cellar air. Each man's face showed the exhaustion of their task and the frustration each night presented.

Thane retained a spark of hope, which was rekindled with each sunset, but Ramiel's temperament wasn't so well-suited to their chore, and he chafed at his inability to make any significant progress in the hours they'd spent hunched over ancient scrolls and books.

A sense of desperation filled the room, and Vasilije would have liked to avoid spending any time there, but each Son understood the key to defeating the Archons existed somewhere in those ancient texts and the prophecies of Idolas, the youngest of the eight sons of Navarus and Macaria. Taking a seat next to Thane, he hesitated to interrupt them, but finally said in a low voice, "What can I do?"

A small smile appeared on Thane's face as he looked up to see Vasilije. "I'm afraid we're no further than before. I'm not sure there's anything you can do."

The resignation in his voice struck Vasilije. One of only four vampires still alive believed to possess an ability to crack the true meaning of the Idolas Prophecies and one of the two Sons saddled with the task, Thane appeared almost as an enigma to the other Sons. Made a vampire in Tudor England, he seemed to be of no particular age or era. His one defining feature, his eyes, projected a sense of warmth and kindness so rare among their kind, yet he remained distant from his fellow Sons, friendly when spoken to but silent for the most part. Of all at the monastery, only Sasa had succeeded in drawing him out of his preferred silence.

Vasilije looked across the table at Ramiel, a very different kind of vampire from Thane. Forever enraged it seemed, he barely contained his frustration with the task he'd had thrust upon him by his sire when he'd left the world over a century ago. Black eyes appeared to burn from anger, making Ramiel an odd complement to Thane in their duty to the entire vampire race. Cursed with an unrelenting rage, confinement of the kind he was forced to endure now was truly more punishment than anything else. His long existence as a vampire had been marked with violence, and Vasilije wondered how long one such as he would be held by the restraint of duty, no matter how important that duty was.

"Ramiel, my offer is a standing one."

He nodded but said nothing. Known for having the face of an angel, the expression he now wore was cold and hard.

"We have found some parts of the prophecy we can translate, but as of now, they make no sense," Thane said as he rummaged through the books and papers in front of him.

"That's some progress, at least," Vasilije said, feeling more hope than on any of his past visits there. "Perhaps another head added to the job might help?"

Thane spread a book out in front of them and pointed to a passage written in Greek. "In the end of ages at the twilight of years. They rose to heights as great."

"Fucking riddles leading to more riddles," Ramiel mumbled.

Vasilije couldn't disagree, but he truly hoped the look on Thane's face meant he saw something in these lines that they obviously hadn't. "Still sounds like Greek to me."

"I admit it's not much," Thane said.

"Repeat it and maybe something will make sense," Vasilije said, trying to be helpful.

"In the end of ages at the twilight of years..."

"Not a good start," Ramiel said angrily.

"Do you have any idea what this means, Thane?" Vasilije asked.

Shaking his head, he grimaced. "No, but maybe with the next line it'll make some sense. They rose to heights as great."

The silence in the room when he finished the second line was deafening.

"Let's assume for now we won't know what the hell the first line means until we figure out who *they* are," Ramiel groaned.

"They can only be vampires in general, the Archons, or us," Thane said confidently.

"Or humans."

Thane stared across the table at Ramiel, who seemed to find some rare amusement in their inability to decode even the first two lines. "You're not helping."

"It seems illogical that a vampire prophecy would spend time on humans," Vasilije said. "So which of the other choices do we think work?"

Neither man said anything for a long moment and then Thane finally answered. "Archons."

"So the Archons became powerful. Unfortunately, this is nothing we didn't already know," Vasilije said. "Have you deciphered anything else?"

Thane motioned toward Ramiel. "Read what you've got."

"One born not made will hold the key."

Vasilije took a deep breath and exhaled his frustration. The prophecy's reference to one born and not made was problematic. This very well could refer to a human. On the other hand, it could refer to something many of his kind believed didn't exist anymore, if it ever did. A vampire born to a woman—to a vampire.

"Clear as mud, right? At least this one only has two choices. It's either a human who will hold the key or a born vampire," Ramiel explained.

"Born vampires are believed to have existed because of the eight sons of Navarus and Macaria," Thane said with a hint of optimism in his voice.

"But they were children born from a goddess, Thane. When was the last time that happened?" Vasilije asked.

He didn't want to play the role of devil's advocate, but better to ask these questions now and get them out of the way.

"There are those who believe they were the first but not the last," Thane said with a smile.

Vasilije looked at each man. "Have either of you ever met a born vampire?"

Both shook their heads. For his part, Vasilije wasn't even sure born vampires ever existed in the first place. He'd always considered the story of Navarus and Macaria's children a myth, more symbolic of how vampires came to roam the earth than a literal telling of events.

"But I'd never met a clyten either, Vasilije, and Dante stands with us," Thane replied.

"Ever the optimist, isn't he?" Ramiel said with a grin. "So now all we have to do is translate the rest of these disjointed ideas, figure out what they mean, and find a vampire who was born. Any chance one of us has been holding out? Maybe Saint?"

"No. I was there when he was made vampire. He's not born."

"How does he hold up stuck in the French countryside with a beautiful female?"

"Seems he's a changed man," Vasilije said remembering how he acted toward Solenne.

"And now all of you have been given Teagan back again. Perhaps fortune is on our side," Thane said. "Perhaps this is just the beginning of the Sons' good luck."

THE LIGHTS in Marc Verrater's office were dimmed when Solenne arrived, and even though she wanted more than anything to be safely back home, she worried her absence would arouse suspicion. To fail now would mean disaster for the man she loved, and after waiting for so long to have him back in her life, she wasn't going to let him go without a fight.

There was no sight of Rochelle at her usual perch at the front desk area, so Solenne continued toward her boss's office at the rear of the suite. What sounded like muffled voices told her he was in tonight.

Peaking her head in around the cracked door, she saw Verrater at his desk looking far more relaxed than usual. The door creaked as she stood watching him, and he turned toward her wearing a sinister grin that sent chills down her spine.

"Lena, I've been waiting for you. Come. Sit down."

Solenne hesitated, unnerved by his devilish expression. Why had he been waiting for her? His deep blue eyes watched her, demanding she obey him, and she swallowed hard as she stepped into his office. Each night with him was as frightening as the first.

"Has something happened, sir? I didn't see Rochelle at her desk."

Verrater leaned back in his chair and fondled his black silk tie, stroking it from the knot at his neck all the way down to the tip. "I sent her and the others on an errand."

Something in his voice made it sound edgy. Dangerous. It immediately made her uneasy and everything inside her wanted to run as fast as her legs would take her away from this place. Everything but her heart, that is. Only her heart remembered why she came to this place again and again, forced to endure the pain and humiliation of the Archon.

Struggling to keep her voice even, she asked, "Oh. Do you have any work for me tonight, or would you prefer I waited at Rochelle's desk in case anyone comes in for your assistance?"

"No. Where you are will do just fine."

Solenne understood what he meant, and her stomach dropped at the thought.

"First, I thought we'd have a little talk. How does that sound?"

Verrater smiled and she saw the tips of his long white fangs as his lips pulled back in that same vicious grin he'd worn minutes earlier.

"Yes, sir."

"Lena, I've long believed you and I to be quite alike. You possess a mind I can respect, one that can weigh the consequences and outcomes of one's actions. I can appreciate that in a fellow vampire. Do you understand?"

No, she didn't. While it was true she did have a mind very much like he described, her behavior around him should have told him quite the opposite.

"Thank you, sir."

Unsure what to expect next, she was unnerved when he switched gears to ask about her past. "Tell me about your sire. I'm curious as to whether this ability of yours is innate or the result of a superior sire's training."

Solenne's mind scrambled to recall what lie she'd told about her sire when she'd applied to work in his office. Lucrecia...yes! She'd used the vaguest details of her friendship with her as the basis for her history, sticking to the broad outlines to convince Rochelle she wasn't who she really was.

"My sire is a wonderful woman named Lucrecia. I was truly fortunate to have been turned by such a soul."

The Archon raised one eyebrow in interest and waved his hand for her to continue. The problem was that she wasn't sure where he was leading her with his sudden interest in her background, and something told her one misstep could land her in very dangerous areas.

"She's an ancient, turned in the early days of Rome."

Before she knew it, Verrater's face had turned dark at the mention of Lucrecia as an ancient, and Solenne hastened to add, "But unlike others of her age, she's loyal to the modern ways, sir. I can promise you that."

Seemingly pleased by her assurances, the hardness left his expression, and he closed his eyes, a sign Solenne took to mean she should continue.

"I was made a vampire right after the Great War. Lucrecia was very much a modern woman even then."

Slowly, he opened his eyes and leveled his gaze at her. "And why was that?"

"She took to the new ideas very easily, bobbing her hair, hiking her skirt length, and even smoking."

Solenne had no idea when Verrater had been turned, so she couldn't even guess if he knew anything about the 1920s firsthand. Her description of her friend was in actuality a description of herself before becoming vampire. Lucrecia was very much the picture of a classical woman then and now.

"And she was kind enough to give you her house? A very generous sire too."

Terror raced through Solenne's body at his statement. She may have been unsure how much she'd mentioned concerning her past, but she was absolutely sure she'd never said anything about where she lived. The smug look he wore told her she'd been found out.

It took every ounce of strength she could muster to remain calm, even as the sick feeling of pure fear turned her stomach. "Yes, sir. She has been very generous with me."

Like an animal circling its prey, Verrater stood and walked around his desk to stand behind her. His lean form pressed against the spot between her shoulders and his smooth jaw touched the side of her face.

"Onto those consequences, Solenne."

Fear of what he'd say or do next made her hold her breath and her heart raced wildly, pounding against her chest. "Pardon? Sir?"

"There can be no pardon, dear. But you may still save yourself," he whispered, grazing his teeth along the top of her ear.

Desperate thoughts raced through her mind. If he knew who she was, he knew who she'd been protecting. Was he keeping her there while another assassin was ending Declan's life?

"Does he know what you do when you come here, Solenne? Does he know how much you've given up for him? I doubt he does. No matter. It was all for naught, it seems."

"Sir, please. I can explain."

Verrater slid his hand down the side of her neck and began to drum his long, slim fingers on her collarbone. His breath came in shallow pants near her ear, terrifying her. What would he demand in return for allowing her to live?

"What would you be willing to do to save yourself?

Give yourself to me? Ah, I can feel by the way you stiffen that this frightens you. Not to worry. You will do that, but I require more now."

He slid his lips down the column of her neck to just below her jaw and pushed the points of his teeth against her skin. Staring straight ahead, she focused on a tiny spot on the wall where the white paint had yellowed slightly and waited for the Archon's next words.

"For your deception, you must pay. You've shown yourself to be an enemy of our world. However, I believe there is a worthiness in you. To stay alive, you must prove this worthiness truly exists."

Solenne knew what was to come next. Fighting the tears that welled in her eyes, she listened as he spoke the words that struck her like a fist to her chest.

"It's your life or his. Your choice, dear Solenne."

Verrater buried his teeth into her skin and roughly pulled her blood into his mouth. The pain tore at her, as it always did, but soon she felt none of it, her mind instead focused on the terrible thought of the world without Declan in it and by her own hands.

No longer able to contain her tears, they rolled over her cheeks at the choice the Archon forced her to make. All those years she'd waited to have Declan back in her arms, even willing to debase herself by supplying him with the women he demanded, for a chance to right what had gone wrong so long ago, only to have this be their end.

As the Archon greedily devoured her blood, grunting and slurping noises filled her ears, but Solenne clung to the hope of finding a way to save both Declan and herself. There had to be some way. She couldn't let them take him away!

Verrater lifted his mouth from her neck and returned to his desk, his face still wearing that same cruel grin. "I'm sure your mind is feverishly trying to come up with some way that both your lives may be spared. Try as you might, you won't find one. Our world is embroiled in a war, and he is the enemy who must be destroyed. Whatever feelings you may have for him, ask yourself if they're more important than your life."

"I won't do this. I won't kill him, so just do whatever you plan to do to me now."

"You're wrong, Solenne. You will do this because whether you believe it or not, you're one of us. The desire to live will win out. You're a true vampire, not one who loathes her nature, like he does. But if you choose him, know that he will still die, but by crueler hands."

Verrater finished speaking and in a flash was behind her, holding her in her chair with his hands crushing her shoulders. "You see, dear Solenne, I favor you, so I've chosen to give you a choice in how he dies."

His lips pressed against her neck, but this time he didn't prepare to feed. Solenne closed her eyes and struggled to be free of him, but he was stronger, and her resistance only served to make him angrier. At last, she submitted and prayed that this would be the last time she'd ever feel his hands on her.

When he was finished, he dismissed her with a wave of his hand. His last words echoing in her ears, she stumbled out into the night air, weak from his attack and desperate to return home, hoping she wasn't too late.

SAINT SAT QUIETLY WATCHING Teagan eat, uneasy at the sense of discomfort he felt around the one soul he should feel some connection to. When he'd heard about his brother's death, he'd genuinely wished he'd had that one last chance to speak to him, but now that the chance had presented itself, all he felt was the sting of old hurts anew.

Teagan looked up from his plate and wasted no more time with silence. "As her sire, I can't keep you apart since she can't sire you. I can make it difficult for you, however."

His fists in tight balls, Saint held back the urge to beat the hell out of him. It would be easy. Indulgent and even more addicted to the luxuries the world offered than his sire, his brother would be no match for him.

"Why? Why do that?"

"Or maybe we should reverse the past and I can take her away from you."

So that's what this was going to be. Finally, after a century of silence, they'd clear the air.

"I didn't take anything from you."

His brother's eyes narrowed to angry slits. "She was mine. As my brother, you should have respected that."

"Yours? Solenne isn't an object you can possess. She's a woman with a mind of her own."

Teagan stood and walked into the next room. With his back turned to Saint, he stood looking down at the fireplace and said, "I loved her. You knew that."

"Loved her? You left her alone constantly while you were off siring other vampires and fucking anything in sight."

He spun around and Saint saw the fire in his eyes he remembered from when they were teenagers, but now that fire seemed darker. Angrier.

"She knew what I was when I turned her. I never promised her she'd be the only one."

"And did you know her when you turned her? That she never enjoyed those parties you loved, full of Absinthe and women begging to be fucked?"

Teagan snorted in disgust at Saint's words. "Don't confuse her preferences with yours. She was fine with our life until you showed up."

"Invited. Remember, you invited me here so you could gloat about being a sire?"

"And don't forget that I am her sire. She will obey me. All I have to do is say the word."

Saint stood and faced him. "Why? You don't love her, if you ever did. Why can't you be happy that she loves me, your brother?"

Teagan's eyes flashed pure hatred, and he yelled, "Like you were for me? How's it feel to know the person closest to you is a stranger set to take away something of yours."

"I never took her. She's like me. When you left her, she needed someone—someone like her."

"And then she left you and you became Saint, a vampire who only fucks humans and whose vampires don't care if you live or die."

Teagan's look of disgust hurt more than his words, but Saint stood silently enduring his attack.

"I'd like to think I had something to do with that, Declan. And she'll leave you again this time too."

"You're wrong. I became that man because of her. Love will do that to you, but you wouldn't know about that, would you? I pity you, Teagan. You became just like your sire."

"Who is happily in love with the woman he made vampire. You've never understood the pull a sire has over his vampires because you're just like yours. All I have to do is let nature take hold once again and Solenne is mine."

Saint knew full well how much control a sire could exert over their vampires. And he knew now that Teagan intended to do exactly that with Solenne.

"I'm not the same man you last saw all those years ago, brother. Get in my way with the woman I love, and I'll see what that bitch in New Orleans thought she did really happen."

A noise behind him made Saint turn around to see Solenne staring at the two of them. "What's happening here?"

Teagan pushed past Saint and walked to where Solenne stood. "I was just explaining to my brother how strong the bond between sire and vampire is."

Cringing at the sight of him with his arm around her, Saint stepped toward them but stopped when he saw Solenne turn out of his hold. Standing between them, she looked first at him, her eyes full of sadness, and then at her sire.

"I'm sure Declan understands quite well how strong that bond is. What he also knows is that it isn't absolute."

"Maybe for someone like him, who ignores his vampires, that's the case, but not for us. Even after all these years, I'm still your sire in whatever way I choose."

Solenne shook her head. "Don't do this. I won't let you take him away from me again."

She took a step back and grabbed hold of Saint's hand. Her eyes were wide with tears as she stared up at him. "I made that mistake once. I swear I won't make it again."

"What mistake?"

"She means when I made her give you up last time. If I recall, you made the choice quite easily."

"What choice? You told me you'd kill him if I didn't let him go," she cried. "I won't let you do this again."

Saint's rage grew with each word. His own brother had been the reason for his losing the only woman he'd ever loved, and he threatened her with killing him? The man who stood in front of him truly was a stranger.

He pushed Solenne to his side and took Teagan by the throat. "Tell me you weren't behind those bastards shunning me for ten years! Tell me my own fucking brother wasn't behind taking everything I ever cared about from me!"

Pushed against the wall with Saint's hand pressing on his neck, Teagan rasped, "You broke vampire law. You deserved to pay."

From behind him, Solenne sobbed, "How could you do that? You had him punished for what we did? You promised me when I let him go that he wouldn't be hurt."

"You had me fucking shunned! You sent me to fucking hell!"

The need to punish the one who'd stripped him of everything—love, friends, a brother, his freedom—pressed on Saint's heart, and he became blinded with rage. How many nights had he wished to know who'd turned him into the Archons, never once thinking his own flesh and blood could be the architect of his misery?

It would end tonight.

Saint easily overpowered Teagan and pressed his fingers into the straining cords of his neck, ready to snap it and end his life. His heart raced at the thought of what he was about to do—kill his own brother. As he looked into his eyes, so similar to his own, Solenne tore at his arm and pleaded for him to stop.

Turning to face her, he said, "I'm already wanted by the Archons. Another crime won't matter."

Solenne's eyes were wide with fear. "Don't do this! Please!"

Saint felt Teagan's pulse throb in time with his heartbeat, felt his life in his hands. "Why? Because he's your sire?"

"No. Because I love you and you'll be tortured by the memory of killing your only brother. Don't do this."

The sadness in her voice touched Saint, and all the strength seemed to vanish from his hands. He let them fall from Teagan's neck and stepped back in disgust. "Don't come back here again. The next time, I'll fucking kill you."

16

Solenne stared in horror at the man Teagan had become. Everything she'd admired in him seemed a distant memory, replaced now with a heartless desire for vengeance against the man she loved.

"How could you Teagan? Wasn't it enough that I ended it with him, breaking both our hearts?"

"You were mine. Are mine."

"No. Not anymore. I can never forgive what you've done. You have no claim on me now."

His face twisted in disgust. "Do you think the Archons are going to approve your turning your back on your sire for Declan, a vampire they want dead?"

Unable to believe there wasn't something of the sire she'd known and loved, Solenne touched her hand to the spot above his heart and searched his eyes for any sign of kindness. "I've been a loyal vampire to you, except for this one transgression. You have women around the world, and whatever you felt for me then you haven't felt for years. I can't believe the sire I adored would deprive two hearts he cared for the love they deserve."

For just a moment, she thought she saw a softening of his expression, but instead of answering her, he looked away and then in a blur, he was gone.

Alone, Solenne walked the grounds behind the house searching for Declan. She needed to talk to him, to show him she'd chosen him. In the darkness, she walked the gravel path that wound through hedges and fountains until she found him sitting on the stone bench where they'd shared that first illicit kiss. In the light of the moon, he looked just as he had that night. As she drew closer, she saw deep brown eyes full of pain gazing up at her nearly breaking her heart.

"I never knew, Declan. I had no choice when he found out. He said he'd kill you if I didn't end it. It broke my heart to say goodbye, and when you disappeared, I thought it was because you couldn't stand to be around me."

Closing his eyes, he took a deep breath and hung his head. "I would've never given up. He knew that."

Declan opened his eyes and stared up at the sky. "For so long, I blamed you for what he did. Every night I asked myself why you'd punish me. And every day I laid awake in bed trying to convince myself that I hated you, even as your face haunted me, making the lies I told myself useless."

The pain in his voice nearly strangled the words as he spoke them, and Solenne touched his shoulder wanting so much to take away his sadness. "Please forgive me. I had no choice."

Shaking his head, he stood and faced her. "There's

nothing to forgive. You took me in when none of my vampires were there for me. You suffered bringing me women..."

Declan stopped and lowered himself to his knees. Wrapping his arms around her, he held her to him. "It's you who must forgive me. I was so consumed with hurt when you left me, and I carried that need to hurt you inside me for so long it became who I was."

Solenne ran her hands over the soft growth of hair on his head, unable to speak a word. The man kneeling in front of her, so strong and powerful to everyone else, wanted her forgiveness.

After everything that had happened—how she'd broken his heart making him the hardened soul he'd been for so long—he was asking her to forgive him. How could she deny him? No one else since him had touched her heart the way he had.

Crouching down to kiss him, she cradled his face in her hands. "That's not who you are. I know the rest of the world sees Saint, but I don't. No matter how much hatred you carried, no matter how much rage you show everyone else, I've never doubted the man inside was the Declan I fell in love with."

"You're all I have, Solenne. But years of being alone have taken their toll. The Declan you fell in love with died a long time ago."

Solenne kissed him softly on his cheek and shook her head. "Not dead. Just buried under years of anger. But I've felt that man in your kiss, in the way your hands caress my body when you make love to me."

He slid his hand to the back of her head and pulled her toward him. The lips that had thrilled her with simply a kiss in that very spot that first night pressed against her mouth, and she felt the passion flow from him, exciting her more than she'd ever imagined she'd feel again.

His tongue slid past her lips to mingle with her tongue, sending a jolt of need straight to between her legs as he expertly explored her mouth. Their years apart melted away until it was as if there had been no time between that first kiss and this one.

Soft lips teased hers and left her wanting more when he turned his attention to her neck. Still sore from the Archon's feeding, she froze as Declan dragged his tongue up the column of her neck in one long, sensual stroke and over the spot the Archon had abused.

Sensing the change in her, Declan raised his head and looked into her eyes. "What's wrong?"

The way he asked made it clear he expected her to tell him everything. Tilting her head to hide the evidence of what she'd done, she forced a smile onto her lips. "I would do anything to see you safe."

Declan squinted his eyes slightly and stroked her cheekbone with his thumb. "What happened? What did they make you do?"

Solenne stood from him, but he grabbed her hand and held her next to him. "I did what I had to for you and the Sons."

"Fuck the Sons! I need to know why you pull away when my lips touch your neck."

He looked up at her, his eyes blazing with anger, and she shook her head. "No. You'll do something stupid!"

In a second, he was on his feet in front of her, his

hands holding her shoulders as he stood staring at her impatiently waiting to hear what she dreaded saying.

"Solenne, what did the Archon do to you?"

Quietly, she said, "Nothing I didn't let him do."

Brushing her hair off her shoulder, he moved to use the moonlight to examine her neck. His expression told her he saw the bruises.

As if to alert the world of his intentions, he said in a low voice, "I'll fucking kill him."

"No, Declan! Don't do anything stupid!"

"Solenne, it's not stupid to protect the woman you love. If I'd do it with my own brother, don't you think I'd do it with one of those bastards?"

Tears filled her eyes and for one of the few times in her life, she didn't try to stop them or hide from them. "That's the first time since you got here that you told me you love me."

"Solenne, they've called me Saint for nearly a century because I refused to sleep with any female vampire—not just mine but any female of our kind. Did you doubt that I love you? That I never stopped loving you?"

In his serious tone, she heard the pain he'd suffered all those years. Willing to show him some of what she'd endured, she said, "More than you'll ever know, Declan."

"Well, then I'll have to make it my purpose in life to make sure you know just how loved you are."

This was the Declan she'd fallen in love with, the Declan whose feelings so often seemed hidden, but at those times when they bubbled up to the surface, made him devastatingly charming.

"I like the sound of that."

Taking her by the hand, he led her back along the

path toward the house. "Good. You'll like what I have in mind."

THE SWEET TASTE of Solenne's skin on his tongue made Saint's cock surge against his belly. It took every ounce of willpower he possessed not to sink his teeth into the swell of her full breast and lose himself in her blood. But he wanted this time to be different.

He wanted to show her how much he adored her.

Cupping her breast, he gently sucked the pink tip to an excited peak, careful to let his fangs only graze the tender skin. Solenne whimpered her desire as she arched her back, urging him to give her more.

God, he loved feeling her under him, her body open for him! No woman had made him feel what she did just by being her. The simple touch of her hand on his head, the needy sound that laced her words when he touched her created more happiness in him than a century worth of women.

Tilting his chin up toward her, she said, "Declan, I want to feel you inside me. I want to forget every night between all those years ago and now. Help me forget."

Blue eyes clouded from need and desire silently begged him to hurry, and he slid up her body to cradle her in his arms. "I loved you in spite of myself. It was the only thing I could do. Don't think about all those nights. Think about every night from this moment on in my arms."

Saint kissed her deeply and slid into her waiting body, loving the sensation of her soft walls stretching to take all he offered. With her arms and legs wrapped around him, she clung to him as he thrust into her, burying himself deep inside her.

Her body fit his as if it had been made just for him, like a piece to complete a puzzle long ago left unfinished. She excited every nerve ending in his body with no more than a word or a smile.

How many nights had he closed his eyes and imagined her beneath him as he sought that moment of happiness with a woman—that fleeting moment when he knew he pleased another?

But it was more than that with Solenne. More than physical pleasure. More than knowing his body thrilled hers as much as hers did his. No, when he looked into those ocean blue eyes so full of emotion, he saw a part of himself she'd taken even without him realizing until it was too late.

Every night he'd searched for that missing part, hoping to find it in some small measure in pleasing a woman and accepting that was all he could ever be. Now, whole in her arms again, he understood what real happiness was.

"Declan..."

Solenne smiled up at him sweetly and he slowed his pace. Turning her head, she exposed her neck and whispered, "I want nothing between us. Take from me to show me you trust me to take care of you as you take care of me."

He knew what she meant and hated it. Hated the idea of what she'd done. And loved her all the more for her strength.

Gently, she pulled his head toward the place that

would provide him with her very essence. The feel of her soft skin against his lips reminded him how much she must have suffered at the Archon's hands, and he paused to worship with a kiss that precious gift she offered unconditionally.

Her skin smelled like flowers on a summer morning, as if she'd somehow conquered the curse of their kind and laid down among honeysuckle on a sunny July day. Saint inhaled deeply, savoring the fragrance that reminded him of his life in the Irish countryside.

He pressed his fangs against her skin, feeling her tender skin begin to surrender to their razor-sharp points. Slowly, he entered her, stopping for the briefest moment as he waited for her body to deliver her sweet blood. It hit his tongue and a wave of excitement raced through his body, making his limbs heavy and his cock surge inside her.

Her blood flowed down his throat, making his body come alive like only blood from her could. Each pull on her vein brought him closer to release, and he fought to control urges that threatened to overtake him.

Closing the holes, he lifted his mouth from her neck and groaned, "Solenne, ride me and take what you need."

Saint slid out of her and rolled onto his back, happy to wrestle some control from his animal urges that threatened to make him no better than the fucking Archon. Thankfully, Solenne sensed none of his thoughts and climbed on top of him to straddle his hips.

Perched atop him like a conqueror, she leaned down and threaded her fingers through his. With his hands pressed above him, he waited, willing to relinquish the power to her.

Her soft hair dangled in his face, tickling his lips, as she rolled her hips to create friction against his cock. Over and over, she slide her wet folds up and down his shaft, almost taking him inside her but each time deliberately allowing only the head of his cock to enter before she rolled back to begin her teasing again.

Let other males have those sweet, submissive types. He preferred a woman who was his equal any night.

Solenne licked her lips and as her gaze roamed over his body, a devilish grin slowly spread across her face. "All these muscles and here I sit with all the power. You might put all those hours in the gym to better use."

"Have anything in mind?"

Dropping her head, she whispered seductively next to his ear, "A few things."

Her fangs playfully nipped his earlobe as she slid her lips to his neck. Warm breath puffed against his skin, and he waited for her to pierce his vein to take from him.

He wanted to move his hands, to hold her hips as he slid her down his cock, but he liked giving her this. For too long, everything about him had been about control. Control of his emotions. Control of his body. Control to deal with living alone, separate from their world. Giving her the control freed him.

A tiny kiss touched his skin and then she sunk her fangs into his neck. His back arched and his hips lifted off the bed, sending his cock along her moist slit before he buried himself completely inside her. As her mouth sweetly sucked what she needed from him, her body fucked his, rhythmically squeezing and releasing his cock until he couldn't hold off the end anymore.

Solenne's moans against his skin told him she was

almost there. Instinct took over, and he broke free from her hold to keep her firmly in place on top of him as she began to come. Her body closed in around him and then his body flooded hers.

He'd never experienced the feeling of pure ecstasy from making love to one of his vampires as he sired her, but he couldn't believe that could be any better than the way he felt when he made love to Solenne.

She tenderly slid her tongue over his skin to close where she'd drunk and lifted her head to kiss him. Her lips, stained a deep red, kissed his lightly. "Declan, go away with me. Anywhere. I'll go anywhere. Please, can we leave here?"

Tucking the hair behind her ears, he saw she was serious. "There's nothing in this world I'd rather do than leave everything and go away with you. Nothing. But we can't. Not now. Not with what the Archons have started. But I promise when this is done, we'll go somewhere and begin our life together."

Solenne said nothing but kissed him and then rolled off him to rest her head on his chest. For a long time, they lay there silently as Saint stroked her back and wondered where they would live after all the bullshit with the Archons was over. Money wasn't an issue. He'd amassed a small fortune over the years. Maybe the States. Maybe Spain. He'd been there once and liked it.

"Declan, no matter what happens, you're the love of my life."

Kissing the top of her head, he smiled and said, "I should hope so. You don't proposition just any man to go away with you to start a new life, do you?"

Solenne lifted her head and stared into his eyes. "No matter what happens, remember what I said."

Cradling her face, he placed a kiss on her lips. "I'm not letting those sterile fucks dust me. I don't care who they send. They can send all my vampires who hate me. I'm going to be on Earth for a long time and you're going to be with me. All those hours in the gym weren't for nothing."

17

Saint felt the approach of the dawn settle into his body, but the last thing he wanted to do was rest. Making love all day sounded like a better idea. As he considered whether to join Solenne in the shower or wait for her to return to their bed, the doorbell chimed, and he reluctantly slipped on pants and made his way to the front door.

Opening the door, he saw Vasilije, Terek, and Dante staring in surprise at him. He was definitely not in the mood for this.

"Don't you have women to keep you busy? It's almost dawn."

"Odd question coming from you," Dante said in his usual smart-ass tone.

Saint's fangs snapped into his mouth, and he growled his displeasure.

Vasilije stepped forward, his face far more serious than the young vampire's. "We need to see Solenne."

Shaking his head, Saint stood toe-to-toe with the

Romanian. No way was he letting this group in to ply her for information. "No. I'll have her call you tonight."

"This can't wait, Saint. We need to see her now," Terek said from behind Vasilije.

Great. Now they had the mystical guy he actually didn't mind making their case.

"What's so fucking important that you feel the need to ruin the last few hours of night to see my..." Hesitating, Saint quickly decided none of them needed to know what she was to him.

From behind him, he heard Solenne ask, "Declan, who are you talking to?"

His gaze traveled from one man to the next. "Vampires who've forgotten what time it is."

Solenne slid her arms around his waist and peaked around his shoulder. "Hi guys. Hi Dante! It's nice to see you again."

"They were just leaving."

"We need to speak to you, Solenne. Back at the monastery would be better."

Before she could answer, too nicely he was sure, Saint moved to close the door and put an end to this. "Vasilije, she's not going anywhere with you."

"Declan, let them in. They're trying to protect you like I am."

"Then let them do it tonight."

"This can't wait. Don't make this difficult," Vasilije said way too close to his face.

"I'm not my brother, Vasilije. I'm not one of your vampires, so if I choose to be difficult, you'll have to fucking deal with it. I won't say it again. Come back later."

Solenne pressed her cheek to his back and hugged

him. "Declan, we have the rest of our lives to be together. This sounds important."

Looking over his shoulder, he saw her looking up at him with those blue eyes that never failed to touch him. Damn, he couldn't say no when she looked at him like that.

Turning back to the three men about to intrude on them, he let his smile fade to a scowl. "Fine but make it quick."

As they filed past him, he turned to Solenne to sneak a kiss. "Don't let him convince you to keep working as a spy at Verrater's. He can find someone else."

Solenne ran her hands over his chest, letting them settle just above the waist of his pants at his hipbones. "When they leave, I have this thing I want to try that Sasa told me about. You game?"

The way she raised her eyebrows made him think he was definitely game. "Vasilije better hurry," he whispered near her lips.

SAINT FOLLOWED Solenne into the sitting room and stood behind her when she sat. "Let's get this over with. And if this is about her doing any more spying or anything to do with Teagan, the answer is no."

The three men sat down facing Solenne, and Vasilije spoke first. Immediately, Saint disliked his tone.

"We have some questions about what you've done with the Archon, Solenne."

"What the fuck do you mean you have some questions about what she's done?"

Vasilije looked up toward him. "Maybe you shouldn't be here for this, Saint."

"Who the fuck do you think you're talking to? I told you I wasn't interested in following you. I'm a Son because of the Order, not you. And you're in her house as a fucking guest who's quickly wearing out his welcome."

Terek hastily moved to diffuse the mounting tension. "Saint, I think what Vasilije meant was that perhaps Solenne would prefer if you weren't to hear what she's done in aiding you."

"I know what Solenne's been forced to do, Terek. That's why she's not going back there. Whatever you have to say, you can say in front of me."

Saint placed his hand on her shoulder to ensure they understood his point. Solenne was the woman he loved, and if they had something to say to her, they would say it with him present.

"It's your choice, Saint," Vasilije said somberly. "Solenne, I need to know what your relationship is to the Archon."

Saint set his jaw and worked to not take Vasilije apart piece by piece. Relationship? What the hell was he talking about?

Solenne didn't seem to understand what he meant either. "We don't have a relationship other than my spying on him for the Sons. Why are you asking me this?"

The three men sat silently, and Saint repeated her question. "Why ask her this? Someone offers us help and goes through what she's had to at his hands to protect me, and you come here with your version of the Inquisition?"

"We've heard some things and we just want to

straighten them out. Saint's safety is our only concern, Solenne."

"Vasilije, I would never do anything to harm Declan. Never. Ask whatever you want."

Saint waited to hear what these things they'd heard were. Did Teagan have something to do with all this?

"Solenne, has the Archon ever had your blood?" Vasilije asked.

Saint threw up his hands, fed up with entire situation. "That's it. We're done here."

As he moved to show the Romanian how unwelcome he was, Solenne grabbed his arm to stop him. "Don't, Declan. I want to answer the question."

Saint shook his head. "No. You don't have to do this."

"I want to. I've done what I thought was right to keep you safe. And I'd do it again, so if they need to hear it, so be it."

He watched her square her shoulders and sit as straight as can be in her chair. More than anything else, at that moment he admired her strength. Turning back toward his fellow Sons, he felt a surge of pride for the woman next to him. "You're fucking lucky she's who she is and that I respect her choices."

"To answer your question, yes, he's had my blood. I needed him to trust me and when he demanded I allow him to have it, I didn't feel like I had a choice. Verrater is cruel, like all Archons, but he seems to love inflicting pain when he takes my blood."

Solenne turned her face away from them and pulled her hair back from her neck to show a painful looking bruise. "This is the result of the last time he took from me."

Saint looked down at the deep purple mark and felt his blood run cold. The thought of that motherfucker hurting her and enjoying it made him seethe. When he got his hands on him, he'd know pain.

Vasilije and Dante stared at the evidence of Verrater's cruelty, saying nothing, but Terek seemed particularly affected by what Solenne had endured. "I'm sorry you've suffered to help our cause. We are in your debt."

Terek's green eyes reflected his genuine concern, and Saint appreciated at least one of them seemed to understand what she'd given up for them.

"Solenne, we don't want to upset you, but these next questions must be asked," Vasilije continued.

"I have nothing to hide. Ask whatever you must."

Vasilije took a deep breath and asked, "Have you slept with him?"

Saint balled his lowered hand into a tight fist as the words left Vasilije's mouth. He had no way of knowing if she had, but he'd suspected it. The idea made him sick, especially because if she had slept with him, it had been to protect him and had likely been tantamount to rape.

"That's enough. Solenne is the victim here, not the bad guy. She deserves better than this bullshit."

Solenne covered his hand with hers and turned to face him. Her eyes were wide with fear, telegraphing her answer without her having to say a word. It didn't matter. He'd have to live with his jealousy. This was the woman he'd loved for nearly a hundred years. If she'd done anything with the Archon, she'd done it to protect him.

"I'm sorry, Declan. I wanted to tell you, but it never seemed like the right time. Please understand."

As she spoke, she squeezed his hand and he felt her

begin to tremble. "I don't blame you. I meant what I said. You're the victim. And I'm the last soul with any right to pass judgment here. You've done what you did to protect me. I'm the one who's sorry."

Saint smiled down at her beautiful face and hoped she knew how much he loved her. Whatever she'd done, he'd have to deal with it.

And when he found that fucking Archon, pain would be the least of his problems.

Solenne forced a tiny smile that told him she understood and turned back to face the three others. "Not that it's any of your goddamned business, but yes, I slept with him for the same reason I let him have my blood—to help protect the man I love, the man I've loved for a century. You told me you needed me to spy on Verrater. Well, you served me up like a sacrificial lamb. He's a sadist who treated me like his sex slave. What was I supposed to do? Refuse him? Then I'd never have a chance to find out anything about what their plans are for Declan or any of you."

"I'm sorry, Solenne. I knew nothing of Verrater when I told you to spy on him. And I never expected you to sacrifice yourself to help us," Vasilije said quietly.

"I didn't do it for you. I did it for Declan."

Saint had heard enough. "She answered your questions. It's time for you to go."

"I only have one more, Saint. Solenne, did you ever take any of Verrater's blood."

Finally, Saint saw where their questions were leading. They thought Solenne had betrayed them and was playing him.

"Vasilije, why would you ask me that?" Solenne asked, her voice shaky.

"Because we've had a report that you have and Verrater has chosen you to be Saint's assassin."

"No! That's not true! Well, part of it is. He did tell me I had to kill Declan, but I would never do that. I couldn't! You have to believe me. I never took his blood. To do that and sex would mean I'm his. Never! You have to believe me."

Saint stood stunned for a moment as the news of what Solenne had been shouldering all on her own sunk in. As she turned to face him, he saw the toll Vasilije's questions and the Archon's command had taken on her. Her eyes, filled with tears, searched his face for some sign he still believed in her. Taking her in his arms, he held her tight.

"You're one class act, Vasilije. She told you what you wanted to know, so get the fuck out. You three know where the door is."

Solenne quietly sobbed against his chest as Saint stroked her back. As he led her to toward his room, Vasilije asked, "How long have you known Marc Verrater, Solenne? Is he the one you left Saint for all those years ago?"

Saint's limbs felt like led at the sound of the name Marc. A memory buried for so long was suddenly unearthed and exposed to the world. Solenne looked up at him in horror, understanding Vasilije's words instantly.

"No! You're wrong!" she cried.

"Are you saying you didn't leave him for someone named Marc?"

Solenne grasped at his arm as Saint backed away

from her. "No, you don't understand. Declan, it's not what they're saying. Please! Listen to me. Don't listen to him!"

"We have the letter you wrote him saying you were leaving him. Marc was the man's name."

Solenne's eyes pleaded for Saint to believe her, but everything seemed to swim in front of his eyes as she reached out to take him in her arms.

"Declan, don't do this! Don't believe them. It's not what it seems. Declan!"

Saint pressed his back to the wall, sure if he didn't he'd slump to the ground. Every word Vasilije uttered brought back the pain of losing Solenne and his punishment soon after, and every word that came from her mouth inflicted new pain on top of the old.

"Solenne, we need you to come back to the monastery with us," Terek said as he took her by the arm. "Don't worry."

Tears ran down her cheeks as she frantically struggled to free herself from Terek's hold. Like something from a nightmare, the scene seemed to play out in silent, slow motion in front of Saint. Solenne's outstretched hand reached for him but fell short as she was led away. And then he was alone, consumed by the thought of another betrayal and Teagan's promise that she'd leave him again.

He looked up at the night sky full of clouds that obscured the stars. In minutes, the woman who filled his every waking thought would return to his arms and he would once again taste her on his tongue.

Forced to meet in secret now that Teagan had decided to

return, they cherished every stolen moment, knowing the danger if they were caught. For her, he would've risked sun and stake to once again be buried inside her. For her, he withstood the torture of living in the same house, never able to touch her for fear of putting her in danger.

He watched other couples stroll through the park, out in the open with their affections, and a spark of jealousy ignited inside him. He wanted the world to know how much he loved Solenne, wanted to shout it loud for all to hear, but she wasn't his to love. That privilege fell to his brother, who treated the gift like a task he occasionally remembered to complete.

Minutes turned to an hour, and he began to worry she'd been caught sneaking out to meet him. Teagan's return just a week earlier had been a surprise even to Declan, and since then the only time he shared with Solenne came through stolen moments and always with the risk of Teagan finding out their secret.

The park emptied of people, and he left disappointed and concerned for her safety. As he walked over ancient cobblestones through the old town, he cursed his brother's good fortune of having sired Solenne and his bad.

Vampire law allowed for no reprieve of the sire-vampire relationship as long as the sire wished it to continue. Unfortunately, even though Teagan had chosen to abandon Solenne for all intents and purposes, preferring to enjoy his time with his own sire and as many women as could be accommodated each night, he hadn't formally released her from the physical bond they barely shared.

Declan entered the house, his eyes searching for any sign Solenne had been caught, but he saw nothing to indicate anything out of the ordinary had occurred. On his way to the sitting room, he heard footsteps behind him and turned to see his brother.

"Enjoy your night out, Declan?"

He stared into his brother's eyes wondering if his tone had been intentionally taunting. "Not really a night out. Just went for a walk."

"You should find yourself a woman to sire. I can tell you from repeated experience it's something you'd enjoy."

Nothing Teagan said was on its face proof that he knew anything of where he'd been or who he'd waited to meet, but something inside Declan told him he knew. "I think I'll go to my room now."

He turned to make his way up to his second-floor bedroom, preferring to avoid any more discussion of siring as the only woman he wished to call his own could never truly be his if Teagan continued to hold her to their legal relationship.

On his way, he hoped to see Solenne, but except for Teagan and himself, the house was empty. As he entered his room, he saw on his bed lay a letter. He raised the envelope to his nose and inhaled the familiar scent of flowers that seemed to surround Solenne no matter what time of year it was. Tearing it open, he anxiously pulled the letter out and read the words that tore his heart out.

"Forgive me. I can no longer live a lie. Teagan has released me, and I've met another named Marc. Goodbye."

18

Solenne closed her eyes to avoid the accusatory looks from everyone around her. Vasilije and Dante, joined now by Sion, talked just a few feet away, whispering about her supposed crime and looking at her with sideways glances every few minutes. But closing her eyes only made her feel worse for all she saw was Declan's stunned face frozen in her mind.

"If it's meant to be, it will be."

Turning around, Solenne saw Terek sitting behind her. "Are you the one chosen to guard me? You don't have to bother. I won't go anywhere until they understand what they think is wrong."

Terek stared back at her with green eyes like emeralds shining in the sunlight. His expression was the same he wore all the time—perfectly calm—but his eyes seemed to penetrate her.

"I am not your guard. Think of me more as your advocate here."

"Advocate? Do you believe me that I've done nothing

to harm Declan?" Solenne waited for his answer and then added, "At least not this time."

"I believe you believe you've done nothing against him now."

Solenne turned back in her seat to face those who accused her. Vasilije glanced over at her again and the look of indictment was written all over his face. Crossing her arms, she kept her gaze on his and said to Terek, "I need you to help convince them. Vasilije and Dante are sure I'm guilty."

"Perhaps it's time the truth came out."

Solenne sighed, hunching her shoulders. The truth Terek referred to wasn't just something she could say. Vasilije was her sire's sire and unlikely to want to see him as the man she knew he was. Also unlikely was Teagan admitting he was that man.

"The ties between sire and vampire aren't easily overcome. Why is that not true for you and your sire?"

Turning back to face Terek, she answered, "Because the ties of love for Declan are stronger. Teagan can't accept that. He never could."

The thought of Declan believing she'd betrayed him again made Solenne wince in pain. She had to make the rest of the Sons believe her and then all she could do is hope he would.

"Terek, why do they think I'd turn against Declan and the rest of you?"

"Because you've done it before," Vasilije answered behind her.

Solenne faced forward and met his cold stare with one of her own. "He forgave me. That's all that matters."

"I'm afraid not, love," he said in a voice full of smugness.

"I can understand why he hates you. And just to set the record straight, I didn't do what I did alone. Teagan played his part."

"Your sire isn't the issue here. And you should show more respect for the one who made you."

"God, you can't see anything when it comes to your precious Teagan! Where is he? Bring him here and let him explain what happened back then."

"Unfortunately, for you, he's not here at the moment, so you're on your own, love."

"I'm not one of your women, love, so treat me with more respect."

Solenne turned to Terek, who was quickly becoming her only hope. "I'm guessing you read minds. Tell them what you see in mine. They won't listen to me."

Terek stood from his chair and approached the others. "There are things we don't know that may show you're wrong about Solenne."

Vasilije shook his head in disbelief, but Terek's words had some effect on Dante and Sion whose faces showed interest in the idea that she might not be guilty of the crimes Vasilije seemed so sure she'd committed.

"Like what?" Dante asked.

"Vasilije, your vampire seems to be far different when it comes to his brother."

"What does this have to do with Teagan? If anything, he was the victim of this one's treachery."

"Why did you want me to work with you, risking my life to spy on Verrater, if you think of me like that?"

"I didn't know of your past until recently, love."

Solenne leaped out of her chair in exasperation. "Of course! Teagan comes back from the dead and can't wait to tell you about my treachery, as you call it."

"Vasilije, why would he tell you that?" Terek asked.

"He's concerned about Saint's safety."

That was too much for Solenne to handle. "Are you kidding? Do you even know your vampire? He hates Declan. He couldn't give a damn about his safety!"

Terek placed his hand on her shoulder. "We've obviously got a problem here. Did Teagan accuse his own vampire of working with the Archons?"

Shaking his head, Vasilije explained, "No. He merely expressed concern that Saint had obviously become quite close to Solenne since going to her house."

"And two people who have loved each other for years shouldn't find happiness together, even in times like this?"

Dante cleared his throat to get everyone's attention. "I'm confused. I thought Saint only liked human females."

Solenne sat down in the chair and hung her head. "That's because of me. I admit I hurt him then, but I didn't do it because I wanted to. Teagan found out about us and forced me to break it off with him."

"As he should have," Vasilije chimed in. "You were his at the time."

Looking up, she saw his blue eyes flashing his condemnation of her behavior. "Vasilije, we can't help who we fall in love with. Did you choose to fall for Sasa? I fell in love with Declan and I'm sorry Teagan got hurt. But that doesn't excuse what he did to his brother when he turned him in to the Archon for interfering in a sire's relationship. He had his own brother shunned to punish him for loving me."

Vasilije stepped back in surprise but didn't argue against what she'd claimed. She saw in his eyes somewhere deep inside he knew she wasn't lying.

"He spent ten years away from our world, shunned because Teagan needed to hurt him because I loved him. He tore us apart, threatened me that if I didn't write that letter that he'd kill Declan. I had no choice. I thought he'd be satisfied, but he wasn't."

"Vasilije, she doesn't want to hurt Saint. Let her go home," Terek said to Solenne's relief.

Seated behind his desk, Vasilije dialed the phone. "I need to know Saint's safe." Someone on the other end answered as he put the phone on speaker. "How's it shakin', Vasilije? What can I do for you?"

"I want you to go to Solenne's house in Valence and make sure Saint's okay. Let me know if you see anything suspicious."

Solenne listened to the conversation, sure she'd heard the man's voice before but unable to place it. The fact that someone was making sure the Archon wouldn't get to him made her feel better, but unless he planned to give him his blood, she needed to get back home before sunrise, or she'd be forced to wait until nightfall. And Declan would too.

Vasilije hung up the phone and walked around the desk. "Dante, I want you to keep an eye on Solenne's house during the day. Someone's gone to a lot of trouble to convince Arnie that Solenne is the one who'll get Saint."

Solenne's mouth dropped open in surprise. Dante was a clyten?

Dante saw her shock and winked. "Your boyfriend's not the only interesting one of us. Don't worry. If I see anything fishy, I'll take care of it. I like to ride him, but it's all in good fun."

"All this doesn't change the fact that Solenne's supposed to kill Saint for the Archon. That's still a problem," Terek said, reminding her that even if she was back in the Sons' good graces, she still had to figure out what to do about Verrater's order.

Vasilije nodded in agreement. "Solenne, I think it's time you two left Valence."

"Great. You make him hate me, make him think I'm his personal Mata Hari, and now you think we should go away together. I'll be lucky if he ever wants to see me again."

Dante smiled at her. "Trust me. He'll want to see you again. You're the only one I've ever seen him happy around, if what he shows us can be called happy. But something tells me when we're not around, he's a much nicer Saint."

"Perhaps I should contact one of my vampires and arrange somewhere for the two of you to stay. Do you like warm or cold climates?"

Solenne thought about Terek's question and closed her eyes to imagine Declan on a gorgeous white sandy beach just after sunset. The thought of making love right there on the sand made her smile. Opening her eyes, she said, "Warm."

Now if only she could get him to speak to her again.

"Warm it is. And have some faith."

"That's easy for a former monk to say."

Terek leaned in toward her and whispered close to her ear, "Not as easy as you'd think."

As THE SONS discussed who could be behind the web of lies and misconceptions aimed at making Solenne look the part of the villain, she remembered the time when she'd been just that.

Teagan held her arm tightly, crushing her wrist in his hand. Tears welled in her eyes from the pain as it radiated through her fingers and toward her elbow.

"Going somewhere, my love?"

His voice sounded hollow, as if the one who'd asked the question was devoid of emotion. But Solenne saw clearly from her sire's stare that he was enraged. And calling her "my love" only signaled his belief that she was his to do with as he wished.

No matter how much it harmed her.

"I thought I'd go for a walk," she answered, wincing from the pain his grip on her continued to inflict.

"Alone?"

Solenne knew he'd found out about her and Declan. She had no idea how. Since he'd returned, they hadn't spent more than minutes in one another's company, with both of them careful to show nothing of their feelings. No lingering glances had been exchanged. No behavior that would make anyone believe they were more than mere co-inhabitants in her house.

But somehow Teagan knew. Solenne felt it deep inside.

Maybe it was for the better. Lying about her feelings for Declan made her feel wrong. She wanted to yell that she loved him from the rooftops, not skulk around like a thief in the night. She longed to reach for his hand when he stood close to her, feeling its strength envelop her own as it cradled it protectively. She wanted to lean in next to his ear, not matter who was near, and whisper how she loved him.

"Please let go of my arm, Teagan. You're hurting me."

Teagan's eyes grew wide for just a moment and then he squinted angrily at her. "And just how much do you think you've hurt me?"

"I never meant..." she began and then stopped as his face began to show the true emotion he'd concealed.

"You never meant to make a fool of me with my own brother? Or did you never mean to break vampire law and disobey your sire?"

Solenne lowered her gaze to the floor to avoid the anger in his eyes, but Teagan roughly pushed her chin up to force her to face his questions.

"Please, Teagan. It was never anything we planned."

Releasing her wrist from his iron grip, he cradled her face in his hands. The rage in his expression frightened her, and she closed her eyes in the hopes of blocking out the vision of such anger.

"Open your eyes, sweetheart. It's time to face your crimes."

Eyes open, she forced herself to not look away. No matter what he said, no matter what he did to her, what she and Declan had done wasn't a crime and she wouldn't cower as if she were guilty.

"Where is your co-conspirator now, Solenne? Waiting for you in the shadows somewhere to rendezvous?"

Solenne remained silent, knowing Declan would soon begin to wonder where she was when she didn't show up at the park.

"No answer? Let me guess. A cafe? No, that's not my brother's style. Too busy. Somewhere on the grounds? No, at least not while I'm here, but I imagine when I'm gone, he's fucked you up and down these beautiful gardens."

She tried to shake her head, but Teagan's hands held her face firmly straight ahead. "Don't do this. Please, Teagan."

"But since I'm here, he'd want somewhere as beautiful as our grounds but away from here, of course." Stroking her cheekbone with his thumb, he paused and smiled. "Perhaps a park, my love?"

Solenne's eyes opened wide, and she knew her expression had guilt written all over it. He knew, and obviously for longer than either she or Declan had suspected.

"Your face tells me what I already knew. Did you honestly believe I wouldn't find out? Neither of you would be a very good poker player. Would you like to know your tell, Solenne? What gave you away?"

"Teagan, it isn't how you think. We didn't mean for this to happen."

"Your tell, my love, is that you leave a room every time he enters. You've never been a very good liar, have you? You didn't think I'd notice one day you couldn't even be in the same room as my brother?"

Declan had warned her that her behavior would appear odd, but she couldn't help it. Every moment the three of them spent together held the danger she'd make a mistake and let something slip.

Teagan dropped his hands from her face and smiled. "I think it's time for you to go, love."

"Go?" she asked quietly, stepping back until she felt the wall behind her.

"Yes, go. However, first you need to write a letter. Sit down at your desk, Solenne."

She cautiously moved toward the desk beneath the window and sat down, taking a piece of stationery from the drawer. Gripping the pen tightly as she waited for him to speak, her hand shook, splattering ink across the page. What was she to write? A confession? She would. She'd do whatever he required to be with the man she loved.

He moved behind her and placed his hands heavily on her shoulders. Leaning down next to her ear, he pressed his lips to her cheek. His warm breath touched her skin and for a moment, she believed he was the sire she'd loved and adored.

Then he spoke, and her hopes were dashed.

"You're going to write him a letter telling him I've released you from our bond and you've left to be with another. Pick a German name. It will add a nice touch that will kill him."

Solenne turned to face him, never more afraid in her life. "No! I can't do that to him."

"You can't do that to him?" he bellowed so loudly her ears rang. "You will or it's his death sentence."

"No, Teagan. No! Please don't do this. He's your brother! Take your anger out on me. I'm to blame, not him. He only meant to comfort me when you left me alone."

"Write or he dies. It's that simple, love."

"Why are you doing this? You don't want me anymore. You're rarely here. I'm always alone while you're out with other women. You don't love me anymore."

"You're mine, Solenne. My vampire. Mine. If and when I decide our bond is broken, then you'll be free."

"But he won't forgive me if I do this. You know him. And then you'll release me, and I'll be alone. Is that what you plan to do?"

"Write, or I swear to God, Solenne, he won't live to see another night."

She had no choice. He'd kill Declan if she didn't write the words that would break his heart. With each stroke of the pen, tears rolled down her cheeks and chin. Every word was a lie, every scratch of the point against the paper like a gouge out of her heart.

Finally, she finished and laid her pen on the desk, knowing when Declan read the words that they'd break his heart. Teagan reached over her shoulder and snatched the paper from the desk. Behind her, she heard him read the letter and she imagined Declan's deep voice as he read her goodbye. Burying her face in her hands, she silently begged forgiveness.

"Perfect. You'll be going away for a while. I'll let you know when you can return."

"So now you take my home from me too?"

"This will always be your home, Solenne. Get ready. It's time to go. Lucrecia is waiting for you in Nice."

Solenne closed her eyes at the memory of her cowardice. She'd hurt the man she loved for nothing. And now after all their years apart, after finally getting another chance, he believed she'd betrayed him again.

19

Saint paced the floor as his mind raced with the thought that he'd been a sucker again. Over and over, the words she'd used the first time she'd betrayed him repeated in his head. And now she hadn't planned on merely betraying him. This time she'd intended on seeing him dead.

His chest felt hollow as if there was nothing left where his heart should be. Even if someone tried to stake him, they'd fail. There was only emptiness there now.

The walls felt like they were closing in on him with each pass he made. He should just leave this house—her house—and escape into the night, leaving behind the memory of her and the Sons. What good could he do for them anyway? None of his vampires had come to help him. He was useless to the rest of the Sons. Even worse, he was a liability likely to get someone staked.

Exhausted from emotionally beating himself up over Solenne, he leaned against the wall and closed his eyes, hoping to silence the voice in his head torturing him.

When it finally stopped, it was only because it had been replaced by the memory of her under him as he made love to her just hours earlier.

Fuck! How many years had it taken for him to accept losing her and now he was back to right where he'd been in those first days after being shunned? He'd sworn he'd never let himself feel like that again, but here he was tied up in knots over the same woman.

"You look like shit. Is this what love does to you?"

Saint opened his eyes to see Teagan standing at the other end of the hallway. God, he didn't need this now.

"Get the fuck out of my sight. Don't force me to carry out my threat."

Turning away, he took a step but stopped when Teagan spoke again. "She's going to be the end of you, Declan."

"You released her for another man but not me, your own brother? I can't decide who you cared less for, her or me."

Saint watched as his brother threw his head back and laughed. "You mean Marc? He never existed. Fuck, Declan. I can read you like a book. Always could. I knew the German thing would bother you."

His head spinning, Saint worked to process what he'd just heard. Marc had never existed?

"Then who did she leave me for?"

"Me."

A sharp pain shot through Saint's head as rage exploded through his veins. Teagan stood before him telling him that Solenne had been forced to lie to him— to betray him—for his brother, a man who didn't love her.

God, he'd been such as ass! He'd been so willing to believe Solenne would betray him again he'd let himself be swayed by a ghost from the past. From the start there had only been one villain.

Teagan.

"All water under the bridge now, brother. You and Solenne have once again found each other and love. And although I could stand in your way, I've decided to be gracious and step aside."

Saint moved toward his brother, for the moment containing the urge to take out his hatred on the only family he had left in this world. "Only after convincing your fucking sire that she'd betrayed me again, this time for the goddamned Archon."

Teagan's face lost its smug expression, and a look of confusion came over him. His attempt at feigning ignorance was too much for Saint, whose fist shot out, connecting squarely with his brother's jaw. The force threw him backwards, and he landed against the wall, stunned.

"So now you come here acting like I should be thankful for what you should've given a century ago while Solenne must explain the lie you forced her to tell?"

Before Teagan could say a thing, Saint's fist connected with his face again, jarring his head into the wall and drawing blood that began to roll down his chin. For so long he'd waited to hurt someone to make up for what he'd endured—losing Solenne, being shunned, being unable to be the sire he should've been, losing his brother to the fucking Archons.

Saint stalked Teagan as he scrambled to gather his wits, trapping him between his body and the wall. Eyes full of fear and confusion stared back at him, and for a moment Saint was a boy and older brother back in the Irish countryside. Teagan's dark eyes, so similar to his own and their mother's, reminded him of the promise he'd made to her. That day, as they set out for the first time as men off to war but truly still boys, played in his mind, and his rage ebbed as memories and their warmth replaced it in his heart.

"I can't do this," he mumbled and slowly backed away. "Just get the fuck out."

Exhausted, Saint leaned against the wall. The vision of Solenne's terrified face as Vasilije led her away hours earlier was all he saw. He'd been a fool to so easily cast her aside. How hurt she must have been as she reached out to him only to see him turn away, refusing to even look at her!

He'd make it up to her. They'd overcome everything fate had done to keep them apart. They'd overcome this too.

Opening his eyes, Saint saw his brother lunge at him and in seconds he was on his back, Teagan's fists pummeling his face, evidence his brother's rage still lived within him.

"Can't do this? This has been postponed too long," he yelled.

His punches cut Saint's lower lip, drawing blood, and stunned he swiped his tongue over it, tasting its familiar tang. The sensation of blood on his tongue, even his own, sent his fangs shooting into his mouth and that nature he'd fought for so long took over.

Rolling him over onto the floor, Saint pressed hard

into his shoulders and looked down into his eyes, no longer an older brother sworn to protect him.

Now he was a vampire.

"So true. Postponed from that night you told me of Solenne's love for a man who never existed. From ten years when I wandered alone in the human world, nearly dying without the blood of my own kind. From nights ago, when you came back from the dead thinking you'd take her away again."

Teagan's fangs flashed as he grinned up at him. "Then we finally do this," he said, his voice matching the sneer he wore.

Fuck, he wanted to wipe that sneer from his face!

The first punch hit his jaw and as Saint drew back his hand for the next, his fingers caught on Teagan's fang, slicing the skin. The sting from the open cut intensified as his fist pushed through the air toward his brother's face once more, this time striking his cheek with such force he felt bones crack beneath his hand.

Teagan cried out in agony, like a wounded animal, his eyes flashing his need to inflict the same pain on his attacker. But his anger was no match for the pent up feelings of rage and resentment Saint had held in for so long. Over and over, he took out the years of pain that had haunted him on the one who had been the architect of his suffering.

"Declan! Stop!"

From behind him, Solenne sounded like she was miles away as she screamed his name again, breaking the violent trance that controlled him. Beneath him, his brother lay still, his face bloodied and swollen.

Solenne lightly touched Saint's shoulder, and he looked up into her soft eyes. "Let him be."

Everything that had consumed him seemed to drain out of his tired body at the sound of her words. Slowly, he rose to take her into his arms, desperate for the feel of her against him. Solenne held him tightly, her head on his chest, and he relished the happiness such a small action could bring.

"What they said wasn't true. There never was a Marc. I never took the Archon's blood. Never."

Saint heard the honesty in her voice and lightly pressed a kiss on the top of her head. "I know. I should have always known. I'm sorry I didn't."

Turning her face up toward his, she smiled. "Is he going to be okay?"

Teagan groaned quietly below them. Already his face looked better, his natural healing as a vampire working to help him return to normal.

"Jesus Christ! Saint...dude, what happened?"

Dante stood staring down at Teagan's still battered face not quite yet back to its usual look and the blood stain on the floor nearby. "Did he attack you?"

Saint shook his head. "Take him to the Romanian. Some of his sire's blood will do wonders for him."

Dante raised his eyebrows in a look of disbelief and turned his attention to Saint and Solenne. "You guys all right, or do you need me to hang out today?"

"He's a clyten, Declan. Did you know this?"

Saint looked at Dante's all-too-confident grin and for just a moment disliked him even more than before. So the kid could walk in the sun. No wonder he was so cocky.

"No, I didn't."

"Yeah, how about that? So I can stay if you need me. Just say the word."

"We're good. It's time you got my brother back to his sire's. And I'd go quickly or he's going to be in even worse shape."

"Not to worry. I'll be back in the monastery before the sun can touch him. I've done this before."

Dante picked Teagan up in his arms and turning back around said to Solenne, "No hard feelings about before? We needed to be sure you weren't out to hurt him."

Saint hoped Dante was referring to their making her return to the monastery for questioning and not something more that might have happened there. He'd hate to have to do what he did to Teagan to Vasilije.

No, that was a lie. He'd love to finally take out some aggression on the Romanian.

"I understand, but I wouldn't do that this time."

Dante held Teagan upright and in a flash they were gone. Solenne pulled Saint to her and kissing him sweetly, asked, "Are you hurt?"

Chuckling, he smiled. "No. It was a bit one-sided. All those hours in the gym."

She backed away from him and her gaze roamed over him, as if to confirm his claim. Her eyes widened when she saw his hands, and she held them up to look at them. Cut and bloodied, they resembled Teagan's face.

"Oh, my God! Declan, your hands!"

Saint looked at them, the weapons he'd used to expel the years of hate and anger he'd held inside him for too long. They throbbed in a dull ache now as she pressed the wounded knuckles to her lips.

"I'm fine, Solenne."

"No, you're not. Come with me," she said firmly as she led him to the bathroom. Leaving him to lean against the sink counter, she started the water and gently placed his left hand under the warm stream. It soothed as it rinsed the blood from his skin, revealing the gashes inflicted by Teagan's fangs.

As she caressed her soapy hands over his, she looked up and asked, "Why did you hit him? Did he say something?"

Saint thought about what answer to give and what he'd always wanted to tell their mother when she'd asked the same question.

"He deserved it."

Solenne stopped washing his right hand and smiled. "Do you feel better now?"

He was struck at how she asked the same question as their mother had asked each time they'd fought as young boys. *Do you feel better now, Declan?*

Every time he'd silently shook his head, guilty for hitting his younger brother even though Teagan had always thrown the first punch from the moment he could make a fist. And every time without fail, their mother had said, *"No matter what happens, he's your brother and you're his. Neither of you can forget that in the end."*

Saint studied Solenne's face, wondering if she expected him to say he didn't feel better now. That would be a lie. He did feel better. Much better. "Yes, I do."

"Good."

Solenne finished cleaning his battered hands and patted them dry with a towel. Cupping them in her hands, she brought them to her lips and gently kissed them. "I was so worried you'd never want to see me again after what Vasilije said."

Saint cradled her beautiful face in his bruised hands. "You're the only woman I've ever loved. No one in my life has ever sacrificed as much as you have to see me safe. I would've hated it if you'd taken Verrater's blood, but I would've had to live with it. Either that or I live without you. I won't do that again."

Leaning in, he kissed her smiling lips, loving the feeling she brought out in him. She was the only woman —the only soul on Earth—who made him weak inside. Just a look from her blue eyes, a gentle touch of her hand on his skin, could do more than that of anyone else in this world. It had taken him a long time to accept that no matter how hard and strong he made himself on the outside, there was one who could get inside him and touch a place few believed ever existed.

Solenne turned her head and pressed a kiss into his palm. Looking back at him, she smiled sweetly. "No matter what happens with Teagan, the Archons, or anyone else, I love you, Declan. I don't care what they throw at us, as long as I know you love me, I can handle anything."

"I love you, Solenne. I always have."

Teasing him, she asked, "Is that the beginning of a smile I see?"

Saint grinned and slid his tongue along his teeth. "You should be careful. Asking a vampire to smile can be dangerous."

The click of Solenne's fangs snapping into place echoed against the bathroom tile. Smiling, she said, "So I've heard."

This was the life he'd longed for all those years alone
—sweet, gentle love with a woman equal to him in the
ways that mattered. Now he did the leading as he took
her hand in his and they walked to his bedroom.

For hours he worshipped her in a way that signaled
his acceptance of their past. She was his—always had
been—but now their lovemaking reflected that, and each
surrendered to the other like they never had before.
When he finally drew the first of her blood into his
mouth, it was unlike anything he'd tasted before. It
excited him, soothed him, nourished his body and soul.

And when they lay quietly in one another's arms as
the day waned outside, Saint knew that he'd finally come
home, not to France or this house but to Solenne.

"Declan, Vasilije wants us to leave here immediately.
Terek says we can stay with some of his vampires,"
Solenne whispered against his chest. "But I'm going to
miss this house."

Lifting her head, she looked at him with sadness in
her eyes. "We'll need to leave tonight."

"Solenne, what do you want to do? You obviously
don't want to leave. You tell me you want to stay, and we'll
stay. To hell with what Vasilije wants. If it takes everything in my power, I'll make sure you're safe if you want
to remain here."

She shook her head and slid up his body to kiss him.
"We have to leave. I don't want our life to be one of
constantly running either, but until you and the Sons
make sure the Archons can't take over every part of our
world, we must do what is needed. As long as we're
together, I don't care where we are."

He knew that was a lie. Solenne loved this house. It

was the place she kept her memories alive all those years, and it was the place she'd stay in for the rest of her life, if she could. Resting her head on his shoulder, she snuggled against him, and he heard her sadness at leaving. "But let's stay right here for just a little while longer."

He could have stayed with her against him for the rest of time. No Sons, Vasilije, Terek, and his vampires. No Archons. Just the two of them alone away from the world.

"So where are Terek's vampires? You make it sound like some kind of vampire commune," Saint joked.

Solenne giggled and Saint wondered if his guess had been closer to the truth than he'd imagined. Was Terek some kind of new age communist?

"I think it's closer to a harem than a commune."

"Harem?" Saint knew Terek had a way with the women, but a harem? "And where is this vampire harem?"

"Spain."

Saint hugged Solenne and kissed her lips. "So we'll go to Terek's in Spain."

It didn't matter where they went as long as Solenne was kept safe.

20

Saint awoke alone and instantly missed Solenne's touch. Still groggy from sleep, he worked to focus his eyes on the clock near the bed.

6:01.

Not fully awake but at least half dressed in a pair of workout pants, he made his way down the stairs to the kitchen, rubbing his closely cropped hair as he walked. A familiar voice made his eyes open wide, and in seconds a rush of adrenaline had him wide awake by the time he entered the room to see Solenne sitting at the table with Teagan.

"What are you doing here?" flew from his mouth before he could stop himself.

Teagan put up his hands. "Wait. Before you hit me again, hear me out. I'm here to apologize."

Saint stood behind Solenne's chair, glaring down at his brother. "Apologize?"

Lowering his hands, Teagan began. "Vasilije talked to

me when Dante took me back to the monastery. I've been a real prick for a long time, Declan. I've told Solenne I'm sorry, and I want to say it to you too."

"So that's it? Vasilije gives you some blood, your face goes back to normal, and now you want to apologize for a lifetime of shit?"

Saint stood waiting for Teagan to answer, convinced there was little point in holding the grudge any longer. He'd gotten what he'd always wanted. He had Solenne's love. Everything else was in the past. Maybe it should stay there.

That didn't mean Teagan should get a free pass for a simple apology, though.

"Uh, yeah. That's about right," Teagan answered.

"Did that work on Solenne? That lifetime of shit affected her too."

Teagan flashed a big smile and looked over at her. "I think Solenne can forgive me, Declan. Think you can?"

Solenne turned in her seat to face him and gave him a hopeful look. "I can forgive him because I have you again."

Saint bent down and kissed her cheek. He didn't want to hold all this hatred in anymore. He had one brother in this world, and even if they were never as close as their mother hoped they'd be, they were still family. "If you can, maybe I can," he whispered. Looking across the table, he said, "Maybe it's time. But fuck up again, and you'll need more than magic Romanian blood to fix you."

"Fair enough," Teagan answered with another big smile. "I guess I can't ask for any more."

"Declan, Teagan was telling me he's planning to return to the United States."

"Yeah, I'm going back to New Orleans and leaving you guys to fight the Archons. But I promised Vasilije I'd keep my eyes open there."

Solenne took Saint's hand in hers and squeezed it. "I told him maybe when everything settles down we could go visit him in New Orleans. I hear it's so much fun there."

She gave him that look that never failed to work on him. Even if he never wanted to go to New Orleans or see Teagan again, he would if it made her happy.

Saint heard the click of the back door and footsteps coming down the short hallway to the kitchen. "Vasilije came with you too?"

Teagan shook his head. "No. He and the two prophecy guys were close to a breakthrough on some parchment, so I came alone."

As the footsteps drew closer, a voice called out, "Declan Collins. You here?"

Saint grabbed Solenne and pulled her toward the other hallway as Teagan followed. "Solenne, do you know who that is?"

Shaking her head, she squeezed his hand tightly. "No, but I think I've heard the voice before. I heard him talking to Vasilije on the phone last night, I think. Declan, you need to get out of here now!"

Teagan nodded and turned to go find the man. "Solenne's right. I'll deal with him. You go."

Solenne grabbed his arm. "No! I've heard that voice before at Verrater's too! He's been at the Archon's when I was there."

"There's no point pretending you're not here, Declan,"

the man called out. "Come out and the girl doesn't have to get hurt. You know how this has to end."

Saint led Solenne and Teagan to the guest bedroom on the main floor. Once inside, he turned to his brother. "Take Solenne out of here now! Get her to the monastery and Terek will get her somewhere safe. Go!"

"No! Declan, don't do this! It's three against one. We can take him," she cried.

Teagan took Solenne's hand and pulled her toward the door. Opening it a crack, he looked out and turned back to face her. "Stay here."

Looking at Saint, he said, "Declan, we're even now. Stay here until it's all clear and I call you out."

Pushing Solenne toward Saint, Teagan ran out into the hallway toward the man's voice.

Solenne's eyes flashed in horror. "Declan! We have to stop him!"

"Stay here. Don't come out until I say so!"

Saint heard the man speak to Teagan, mistaking him for the man he was sent for. Before he reached the end of the hallway, he heard the sound every vampire feared as a stake was plunged into Teagan's heart and then there was nothing but silence. He rounded the corner of the wall and saw his assassin pull the stake from Teagan's chest and then his brother was gone.

He charged the vampire, who stood stunned at the realization he'd staked the wrong brother, tackling him to the ground. Saint's fists smashed into his face, breaking his nose and jaw, but knowing he'd hurt him only made Saint want more. Again and again, he slammed his knuckles into the assassin's face as blood splashed from his mouth and nose, covering Saint's hands.

Finally, when he could hit him no more, he grabbed the stake that had just taken his brother's life and plunged it through the man's chest. In seconds, all that was left of the man was dust on the floor beside Saint.

HOW LONG HE SAT THERE, exhausted from rage and the pain of losing the brother he'd just had returned to him, he didn't know. Time seemed to stop as he stared in utter sadness at the pile of dust that was once Teagan.

Solenne called out from the bedroom, her voice terrified. "Declan? Please answer me! Please let me hear your voice so I know you're still with me."

The fear in her voice shook him from his misery, and he rose to intercept her before she saw the evidence of the two murders. "Solenne, stay where you are."

Always strong-willed, she didn't listen and ran into the room. "Declan, thank God! I heard you hitting that man." Looking past him, she saw the remains of the assassin on the floor.

"Solenne, we need to leave. Come."

"Where's Teagan?"

Solenne looked up at him and tears began to fall from her eyes. "No! Tell me what I felt was wrong. Tell me he's gone back to Vasilije's."

Saint took her in his arms and held her tightly to him as she sobbed. He understood her pain just as she understood his. "We need to go now. It's not safe for you here."

Solenne nodded sadly and looked around at the place that had been her home for almost a hundred years.

"I promise we'll come back," Saint whispered as he pressed his lips to her cheek. If it was the last thing he did on this Earth, he'd make sure Solenne was safe and back home.

SAINT HELD Solenne next to him as they waited for someone to answer the monastery's front door. As long as he got her safely inside, he could know she was out of danger and protected by his fellow Sons. The door opened and Sasa reached for Solenne, taking her into her arms.

"I'm so sorry. Vasilije felt it as soon as it happened. Is he really gone?"

Solenne nodded and began to cry, her tears muffled by Sasa's embrace. Saint stood silently, sharing her grief at Teagan's loss, but inside that sadness began to slowly morph into a hatred that would only be sated by the death of the one responsible for his brother's death.

"Saint, I'm happy to see you and Solenne escaped," Vasilije said quietly from the doorway to a room nearby. Saint said nothing. No words seemed enough.

"Join us. We need to discuss your leaving with Terek."

The usual confident tone of Vasilije's voice was absent, replaced by a somberness that struck Saint. Teagan's death was final this time. No mistake.

Solenne turned to Saint and squeezed his forearm reassuringly. "Go. I can't sit and listen to this now. Sasa's offered me a place to rest for a while. When you're done with them, come find me and we'll go to our new home."

Saint bent down and kissed her lips, wishing he could take even some of her pain away. With his thumb, he wiped the tears from beneath her eyes. "I won't be long. Rest and I'll find you when I'm done."

As Solenne left with Sasa, Saint's hatred for what he'd brought into her life merged with his hatred for the Archon and he knew what he had to do. He walked into Vasilije's study and saw the others waiting for him. "I need to talk to Vasilije alone."

Without a word, they filed out of the room, leaving a sire and brother in mourning. But Saint didn't have time to grieve.

"I need you to make sure Solenne goes with Terek to Spain if I don't get back tonight. She's going to fight you, but I need your word you'll see her away from all this."

Vasilije stared up at him. "I will. Be careful. She can't handle losing you too. And we need you, so don't do anything stupid."

"I don't plan on doing anything other than killing the fucking Archon. I'm done playing cat and mouse games with this motherfucker. He wants me dead? Too fucking bad. I want him dead more."

"What do you want me to tell Solenne?"

"Tell her..." Saint hesitated and then said, "Tell her I'll be back."

THE STREETS of the walled city of Avignon were eerily quiet as Saint marched through them, a vampire on a quest for revenge. Each step he took echoed off the stones underneath his feet. Houses that had seen the march of armies, of death from plagues, stood silently as if abandoned in anticipation of his coming.

Down alleys and side streets he strode, each one taking him closer to his final destination and the end of Marc Verrater. The memory of the bruises on Solenne's pale skin played on his mind, and Saint's rage spiked in him, spurring him on. He knew she'd done what she had to in order to protect him, but that only made it worse. It made him responsible in some way, an idea that sickened him.

But for one of the rare times in his existence, he'd turn his hate outward toward the one who truly deserved it.

A light wind blew in off the Rhône River, chilling the air as Saint at last turned onto the road where he'd find the Archon. The air did nothing to cool him, though, as he took the last steps to the building he sought. Every hurt, every loss he'd take out on the one who symbolized everything he hated about being a vampire.

He'd been to this place before. A lifetime ago, it seemed. A different Archon had stood in judgment of him then, sending him out of the vampire world for ten years. Tonight, he'd be the one meting out the punishment.

The Archon's offices were dark, all except a room at the end of the hallway, where a dim light peaked out from under the door. Saint knew the one he sought was in there. His heart pounding, he turned the knob and opened the door. In front of him sat Marc Verrater. Dressed similarly to Saint, he was much younger than any Archon he'd seen before. For a moment, he stood stunned by the man, who appeared calm, as if he'd expected Saint to come that night.

The Archon stood, showing while he may have looked calm he knew why Saint had come.

"That stupid fuck you sent to kill me is a pile of dust."

A smile crept slowly onto Verrater's face. "Not surprising, but it doesn't change the ultimate outcome. Your kind must be eliminated. The Sons of Navarus. The prophecy can't be fulfilled if you live."

Saint moved toward him. "I hate to disappoint you, but that's not going to happen. You'll be the first Archon to find out what happens when you fuck with us."

The Archon looked past Saint and shrugged. "I see no us. All I see is one."

"This is personal. I'm here for my brother, who that fuck you sent for me staked by mistake, and Solenne."

"Dear Solenne. She disobeyed me by not handling the job herself, so I had to send Arnie."

Saint curled his hands into fists. He was going to enjoy beating the hell out of the Archon before draining him so slowly he begged for mercy. "Don't speak her name. Don't think of her."

The Archon slid his tongue across the seam of his mouth and smacked his lips. "I've done far more than say her name and think about her. She's a rare treat wasted on a vampire who only fucks humans."

His words made something rage inside Saint, and he lunged at the Archon, grabbing him by the throat. The force sent the two of them hurdling toward the far wall, and it stopped Verrater's movement with a loud thud. Saint took advantage of his shock and hit him hard on the jaw, slamming his head into the wall.

Almost as big as Saint, the Archon quickly put up a much stronger fight. Twice he caught Saint in the mouth, drawing blood, and he overpowered him to take him to the ground. Landing on top of him, the Archon's weight crushed against Saint's body as it smashed against the floor.

It had been years since Saint had fought anyone so close his equal, and after the initial shock wore off, he began to relish the chance to humiliate Verrater before taking his life.

The Archon may have been as skilled a fighter, but Saint quickly found his weakness. Unless he was on the offensive, he was unable to fight at all. But he was big and getting him on the defensive wasn't easy.

Finally, Saint maneuvered him under him and began pummeling his face. Each time his fist hit him, a tiny part of the hurt and rage left Saint. It would take far more than what he could do with his fists to rid him of everything that made him hate Verrater, though. No, that release would only come with his death.

Beneath him, the Archon lay bloody and beaten, but Saint needed him to feel more pain. For every time he'd forced himself on Solenne. For every bruise his hands had left on her tender skin. For every drop of blood that he'd taken from her. For every hurt he'd inflicted on the woman he loved and the life he'd taken from his brother.

Saint pulled a rope he'd brought out of his coat and tied Verrater by his hands and feet to his chair. Unable to move, he sat motionless, his head lolling back and forth on his neck.

"I could just stake you, but that wouldn't be enough. I need you to feel pain—pain like the kind you've caused."

Verrater looked up at him, his one eye swollen shut. "You'll never get us all. There are too many of us," he groaned.

"I don't need to hurt all of you tonight. Just you. And we will defeat you bastards."

Saint didn't want to talk anymore. He wanted to make the one who'd hurt those closest to him suffer. Leaning in, he scraped his fangs over the Archon's neck and roughly jammed them into his skin. The agonizing pain was evident in the cries that escaped from the Archon's mouth, but Saint bit down as hard as his teeth allowed and pulled painfully on his vein.

Blood filled Saint's mouth, and he yanked his fangs from Verrater's neck to spit it out on the white tile floor. Over and over, Saint plunged his teeth into the Archon's skin, slowly draining him until the floor around them was covered in blood. Verrater's life hung by a thread, and Saint would be the one to cut that thread.

Saint watched the man in front of him as he desperately clung to life. Never before had he so viciously used his ability as a vampire to hurt another, but even now as he prepared to take the final drops of the Archon's blood from his nearly empty body, Saint's desire to hurt him wasn't sated. He would be the first of many Archons that must die to ensure the vampire world didn't end up like them.

A noise behind him made him turn his head, and before he could react, Saint was charged by two of Verrater's men. Even with adrenaline behind him, he couldn't overpower two of them. Fists seemed to come from everywhere, pounding his face, his chest, his gut until he fell to the floor in a crumpled heap nearly as battered as the Archon.

Though eyes blurry with blood, he saw the one whose fist had first smashed into his mouth lift a stake in the air. Saint braced for the moment it would pierce his heart and send him to dust. Thoughts of Solenne were the last he had—her beautiful eyes so full of love, her kiss that never failed to thrill him, her sacrifice for him that had all been for nothing—and then everything went black.

EPILOGUE

Solenne dug her toes into the white sand, loving the feel of its cool, grainy texture against her skin. The water that had seeped into the sand earlier in the day still remained to dampen her feet, sending a tiny chill over her skin.

The moon sat low in the sky, a deep yellow orb above bathing the beach in pale light. Again and again, she looked up and down the span of sand but saw no one. Each night she waited, against the suggestion of Terek's vampires, sure Declan would come to her, and each night was ended by dawn hastening her inside to wait for another night. For months she'd hoped and waited alone, wondering when fate would ever see fit to grant her the one wish she made on the stars above.

She knew he'd come, no matter what the pitying eyes of Terek's vampires showed they believed. He'd come. She'd waited nearly a century the last time. She'd wait as long this time, if she had to.

Spain had become her home since that night Declan had moved against the Archon. Terek had taken her as he'd promised to somewhere warm, but no sign of Declan had been seen since then. The Sons pretended to believe he still lived, but she knew when she wasn't near they whispered what she refused to believe.

That Declan was gone, lost to the war with the Archons.

A lump formed in her throat at the thought. *No.* She'd know. Even though he wasn't her sire. Even though he wasn't her vampire, sired from her own blood. She'd know because he was hers.

Her love.

Her soul.

Hers.

Solenne scooped a handful of damp sand and let it fall in clumps between her fingers. The dark waves rolled in front of her, marking the passing of time as another night ebbed away from her. Tonight, as she did every night, she'd believed he'd come.

"Declan, where are you?" she whispered toward the night sky and North Star.

"The only place I ever want to be—with the only woman I've ever loved."

Solenne spun around to see him standing behind her, smiling like no time had passed between then. "Where have you been?"

"Still not very good with understanding how a man likes to be welcomed home," he said with a wink.

Even the wet sand that held her feet couldn't keep her from leaping toward him, and Solenne threw her arms around his neck, her joy purer than she'd ever known. "Where? How? I've missed you so much."

Declan's arms enveloped her, pressing her body to

his, and she heard his heart race next to her ear. "I'm sorry I couldn't come to you before. But I'm here now."

Solenne tried to hold back the tears that burned behind her eyelids, but it was no use. Months of loneliness, of being the only one to believe he would ever return to her, finally took their toll and whatever strength she'd had dissolved into nothingness, replaced by the tears running down her cheeks.

In his arms, she sobbed as he softly stroked her hair and back. "I never stopped believing you'd come back to me. Never. Fate couldn't do that to us. Every night I waited, Declan. Every night."

Squeezing her tightly, he kissed the top of her head. "I would never give up, Solenne. No matter what, I had to come back. I walked around for almost a century with an emptiness from not having you near me. I wasn't going to let that happen again."

Lifting her head from his chest, she looked up into those dark eyes she loved and saw something different. "Declan, what is it?"

"Solenne, for so long I hated who I was—hated being vampire. I took it out on everyone around me, alienating those who I should have cared for. I couldn't see the gift Kir had given me that night. I couldn't see that you could never do what I'd believed you'd done. I couldn't see that being a sire meant more than turning one into a vampire. I deserved to be alone."

"No, that's not true. It wasn't all you."

He kissed her softly and continued. "But then I was given a second chance with you that I thought was going to be yanked away that night at Verrater's. And something incredible happened. Just as one of his guards was about to stake me, one of my vampires showed up. That's where I've been all this time. I visited as many as would see me. Not all can forgive me, but some can."

"So that's where you've been?"

Declan cradled her face in his hands and looked into her eyes. "Forgive me, but I couldn't come back to you the way I was. I knew you'd be safe with Terek and his vampires."

Solenne grasped his wrists and shook her head. "I don't care about being safe. I care about you the way you were, the way you are now, any way."

"Well, now you have me always. But until this war with the Archons is won, our lives won't be our own."

"Just promise me that when we're alone each day as we lay in each other's arms that the life we've waited so long to have will be ours and ours alone. Promise me that and I can withstand anything."

Declan kissed her just as he did that first night in the garden at her house and all the things that had kept them apart and all the troubles that lay ahead seemed to fade away.

"I promise."

SOLENNE'S HANDS caressing his tired body made Declan feel like he was finally home. Terek's house may have been full of strangers and the towns and countryside around the grounds were entirely foreign to him, but it didn't matter. As long as Solenne was there, he was home.

The months away from her had been torture, knowing she very well believed him dead at the hands of

Verrater. Each night he told himself this was what he had to do, but it didn't make her absence from his side any easier. Now he intended to make sure she'd be in his life forever.

"Feel better yet? I can massage the front, if you'd like," she teased as she nuzzled his neck.

Rolling over, he pulled her on top of him, loving the feel of her body next to his. But as much as he yearned to make love to her, he had something else on his mind. "I don't ever want to be without you again. Too much of our lives have been spent apart."

Solenne smiled and kissed him sweetly. "Declan, I don't plan to let anything separate us again. Heaven help anyone who tries."

"That's not enough."

Solenne propped herself up on her elbow next to him and gave him a confused look. "What do you mean?"

"I want us to be formally joined. Marry me."

"Marry you?"

"Yes. And I know it's not popular with female vampires these days but agree to wear my mark."

"You know you're asking a modern female to do something perfectly medieval."

"I know. Call me traditional. I hope this modern female will do it anyway."

"I had no idea the man I adore was so old-fashioned."

Declan's heart pounded wildly as he waited for her answer. He knew it was uncommon for female vampires to want to go through the process required to wear the mark of the one they loved. Like a tattoo, his blood would be driven beneath her skin, and she would forever show the world that she was joined to him.

Solenne cradled his face in her hands and looked deep into his eyes. Declan held his breath in anticipation of her words, unable to decipher whether her expression was one of love or indecision about how to tell him no, or worse, that she didn't want to marry someone who'd led the life he had.

"Declan, you know I'd endure anything for you. If my getting the mark will make you happy, I'll willingly wear it to show all who see that I love only you. That my heart is yours and yours alone. Do you plan to get my mark also?"

"So now the modern woman wants me to do the medieval thing?" he said with a grin.

"It only seems fair. Are you worried that the other Sons will think less of you?"

Saint imagined the only one of them who'd have the nerve to say anything would be Dante, and having such a perfect justification to bring the cocky bastard down a peg seemed worth a little ribbing from his fellow vampires. "I don't care what they think. If the woman I love wants me to wear her mark, I do it proudly."

"Good. So about this marriage thing..."

Before he could argue his case, she kissed away any words he could say.

⁓

DECLAN STOOD BEHIND SOLENNE, his fingers caressing the raised mark on the back of her neck that signified she was his vampire, if not by blood then by choice. An elaborate triskelion, the mark had been chosen by Solenne because of its meaning to symbolize the end of their time apart and the beginning of their future together. He bore an identical mark on the same spot on the back of his neck, and just as he'd guessed, Dante had been the only one of them who dared say anything. Declan had enjoyed delivering a little humility to the young vampire. Not much, but enough to let him know his place.

"It was a beautiful ceremony, Solenne," Sasa said as she approached them in the great hall of Terek's house where they waited for the rest of the Sons and Terek's vampires to join them.

"Thank you, Sasa. It was a long time coming."

"I'm afraid Vasilije is going to want to talk about the Archons today, Declan. He was right behind me when he stopped to talk to Terek and Dante, and I think I heard him mention that they've made some real progress with the prophecy back at the monastery."

Declan looked across the hall to see the three men approaching them with intent expressions on their faces. Leaning down, he kissed the side of Solenne's cheek. "No rest for the wicked, it seems. I promise this won't take long, and then we can get back to celebrating."

Solenne turned to look up at him. "I knew what kind of vampire I was marrying when I said yes. This is who we are now. I hope you're okay with me joining you. I want to be a part of your taking down the Archons."

Pride at his wife's strength filled him and he smiled. "I wouldn't have it any other way."

"Sorry to crash the party with business, but Thane and Ramiel have something they need to tell us," Vasilije said as he stopped in front of them. "Terek's library will do. We can talk to them from there."

Vasilije stretched out his arm to take Sasa's hand and

together they walked into the expansive room that Terek called a library. Declan was sure he'd never seen so many books in one place, and from the sound of Dante's whistling behind him, it appeared he wasn't the only one impressed with Terek's collection of books.

As Terek and Vasilije got the rest of the Sons on the phone for a conference call, Declan stood silently beside Solenne as she expressed her amazement with the room. "I thought the library I'd inherited from Lucrecia was extraordinary. This makes the one at my house look like a closet."

Solenne's mention of her house in France reminded Declan of the enemies they'd have to defeat before their life together would be as they'd always dreamed. Hopefully, what Thane and Ramiel had discovered about the prophecy would hasten that day when he and Solenne could just live quietly in the French countryside as two souls in love, the way he'd always wished they could.

"Okay, I've got Thane and Ramiel on and Nico, you there?" Vasilije said from next to the large table they all sat around.

"I'm here, Vasilije. And congratulations, Saint and Solenne. I wish I could've been there to celebrate your big day."

"Thane, let's get started," Vasilije said. "Tell us what you found out."

Declan heard the hope in Vasilije's voice and silently seconded it. The quicker they figured out the Prophecy of Idolas, the quicker they could all get back to their lives. Now that Vasilije had Sasa, he more than ever before seemed to be a man in search of the quiet life.

"Well, first of all, I want everyone to know that

without the Order sending Kali to help translate, Ramiel and I might still be sitting in the monastery cellar stuck on the first few words of the prophecy. Please tell the members of the Order thank you from all of us, Nico."

"Will do, Thane. They'll be happy to hear she's already helping. She's one of the best they have."

"We had the first few lines translated before Vasilije left, so let me begin with them. 'In the end of ages at the twilight of years, they rose to heights as great.' We figured this referred to the Archons' rise to power, so we went on from there. The next line is, 'Who is born not made will hold the key.' This refers to someone we think is a born vampire. So far we don't know who this could be, but at least we know we'll be searching for a key of some sort."

"Do you have any idea where this key could be?" Terek asked.

"Not yet, but Kali knows a great deal more about Greek history than Ramiel or I do, so we hope we can figure this out soon. She and Sion are working on it."

"You said you made a breakthrough. Thane. Tell us about that," Vasilije said.

"Okay. As vampires, we all know about the eight sons of Macaria and Navarus. It's where the need for eight vampires to be Sons of Navarus at all times comes from. Deimos, Erasmos, Haemon, Ianos, Monimos, Origenes, Nikator, and Idolas, the eight sons, are important and we believe, part of the prophecy. Idolas was the one who made the prophecy, remember."

"Okay, so what's the deal with these eight sons of the first vampire?" Dante asked impatiently.

Thane paused a moment and then answered, "It was Kali who remembered hearing this years ago. Idolas was the one child of Macaria and Navarus who wasn't a vampire."

The room fell silent, and Terek nodded. "I remember hearing that centuries ago. That's not a myth, Thane?"

"We don't think so. In fact, from what we can figure out, Idolas was born a seer, not a vampire, like his parents. Different than all his brothers, he was fair haired too. And here's the breakthrough. All of us seem to be descendants of Idolas."

Declan looked around at the rest in the room to see if they were as shocked at what Thane had just said as he was. From the looks on their faces, he wasn't alone in his surprise.

"Are you saying we're all related somehow, Thane?" Dante asked.

"In some strange twist of fate, yes."

"Not strange at all, I think," Nico said from the other line. "It makes perfect sense. The Order chooses the men to serve as Sons of Navarus, and it doesn't seem logical they'd choose just anyone."

Dante looked over at Declan and smiled. "I guess this explains why despite all your problems you're a Son."

For a long time, Declan had wondered why the Order of Macaria had chosen him. He'd always assumed it had something to do with his ability to walk among humans so easily, but this made a hell of a lot more sense.

"There's even more. Since Kali arrived, we've been able to decipher another stanza of the prophecy that we believe relates to the second son, Erasmos. Remember his story? He was the son who was the outsider of the family. He saved the only mortal daughter of Hermes, Desdemona, from a rapist and after that, Hermes loved him like he was his own son."

"I remember that," Solenne said looking back at Declan. "I always liked that story."

"Well, listen to this. 'The son of two fathers, ferried from exile through love.' We think this refers to Erasmos being accepted by his parents after saving Desdemona."

"That's all well and good, but how does this help in understanding how to defeat the Archons? And I'm confused. If Saint is a Son because he's the descendant of Idolas, why wasn't Teagan made a Son?"

"Not all descendants of Idolas can be offered the chance to be a Son, Vasilije," Terek said.

"Actually, I think I can help here," Declan said. "Teagan and I have the same mother, but two different fathers. Our mother was left alone by my natural father before I was born, and she met Teagan's father right after. He brought me up as his own, but he wasn't my father, technically. Teagan never knew, but we weren't full brothers."

"Saint, are you saying you had two fathers?" Thane asked.

"I guess. I never met my real father, but I guess you can say I have two fathers."

"Thane, I think you need to take another look at what you've deciphered so far. What you just read to us sounds like it can apply to Saint as well as Erasmos. Ferried from exile through love? Sound familiar?" Terek asked.

The room fell silent as Terek's words sunk in. If the prophecy told something of each of the current Sons, it may be easier to figure out how to stop the Archons. At least now, it seemed, they weren't dealing with an archaic past but things dealing with the present.

"Terek, you should see Ramiel's face right now. I think this could be the second smile I've ever seen on his face the whole time I've known him."

"Before anyone begins to celebrate not only this breakthrough but Saint and Solenne's wedding, there's something you all need to know," Nico said in a tone that erased the happiness of Thane's. "The Order has heard rumors that the Archons weren't satisfied with just killing one of us at a time. We hear that now they'll be going for a Son and all their vampires from this point on."

Solenne gripped Declan's hand tightly as a somber mood came over the group. From now on, not only was each Son marked for death but every vampire they'd ever sired was too. For someone like Terek, who had thousands of vampires, this meant unless he was able to find a way to protect them all, he was going to see some die because of who he was.

"If there's any bright side I can report, it's this. They're claiming they've already gotten Saint. Your French Archon says he dusted Saint that night in his office. Any idea why he thinks this, Saint?"

"Because he doesn't want anyone to know I nearly drained him dead. His ego is pretty big."

"Well, he's become quite a splash in the Archon community, from what we hear down here. I don't think that's the last we'll hear from him, but at least this means you can rest a little easier."

"Nico, do they know who all of the current Sons are?" Sasa asked.

"I wish I knew the answer to that, Sasa. The Order

hasn't been able to confirm that the Archons know who we all are. All we know is that they believe they got one of the Sons already. Unfortunately, Vasilije, your spy Arnie let them know you're still alive. But thankfully, we're all still alive, so let the Archons say anything they want."

Declan looked over at Vasilije and saw Nico's words had shaken him, but quickly he seemed to shake off any concern.

"Take care of yourselves, and if we find out anything here in Greece, I'll let you all know. Until then, congratulations on the wedding and enjoy the honeymoon," Nico said with a chuckle.

"We'll continue working on our end here at the monastery, and hopefully, we'll have more soon. Now that we have a different angle to tackle and Kali's help, things might come easier," Thane said in his usual hopeful voice before hanging up.

"I think it's time we let the newlyweds begin their honeymoon. We can handle the rest of the meeting without you two, I think," Terek said with a sly smile.

Solenne rose to give him a hug. "Thank you so much for everything, Terek. You and your vampires have been so wonderful to me all those months I was here waiting for Declan, and now you're letting us stay here at your beautiful home even longer. We appreciate it."

Declan saw Terek wink at her as he said, "I told you to have faith it would all work out."

"Thank you for inviting us, Solenne," Sasa said. "It was beautiful, my first vampire wedding."

"We'll give you a few days alone before we bother you again, Saint. If we find out anything before then, I'll let

Terek decide if he needs to let you know," Vasilije said with a grin.

Declan didn't see Terek bothering anyone when it came to a woman, so hopefully, even if Vasilije did call with news, he and Solenne wouldn't have to deal with it anytime soon. After they said their goodbyes, they walked hand in hand through the great hall out into the courtyard. The night was hazy and warm and with Solenne's hand in his, he led her to the room they'd shared since he'd arrived at Terek's.

Closing the door, he saw her standing at the window bathed in the silvery glow of the moonlight. How many nights had he seen her just like that, and yet this night he looked at her as if for the first time.

"What are you thinking?" he asked as he wrapped his arms around her and held her to him.

"I'm thinking that this is nothing like what I'd ever imagined when I dreamed of us together."

Leaning next to her ear, he pressed a soft kiss on her neck. "I know you wish you were back home in France. I promise we'll go back there as soon as we can."

Solenne turned in his arms and looked up at him. Blue eyes full of love stared into his, and smiling, she said, "I do miss my home, but it doesn't matter. All that matters is that we're together. France, Spain, wherever. Home is where you are, Declan."

Kissing her, he let the realization of that truth wash over him. Of all the places he'd traveled in his lifetime, nowhere had ever felt like home without Solenne. Finally, after all those years, he was home.

ABOUT THE AUTHOR

K.M. Scott writes contemporary romance stories of sexy, intense, and unforgettable love. A New York Times and USA Today bestselling author, she's been in love with romance since reading her first romance novel in junior high (she was a very curious girl!). Under her Gabrielle Bisset name, she writes paranormal and historical romance. She lives in Pennsylvania with a herd of animals and when she's not writing can be found reading or feeding her TV addiction.

Be sure to visit K.M.'s Facebook page at **https://www.facebook.com/kmscottauthor** for all the latest on her books, along with giveaways and other goodies! And to hear all the news on K.M. Scott books first, sign up for her newsletter today and be sure to visit her website at **http://www.kmscottbooks.com**

BOOKS BY K.M. SCOTT

HEART OF STONE SERIES

Crash Into Me (Heart of Stone #1)

Fall Into Me (Heart of Stone #2)

Give In To Me (Heart of Stone #3)

Heart of Stone Volume One

Ever After (Heart of Stone #4)

A Heart of Stone Christmas (Heart of Stone #5)

Return To Me (Heart of Stone #6)

Forever With Me (Heart of Stone #7)

Heart of Stone Volume Two

Hard As Stone (Heart of Stone #8)

Set In Stone (Heart of Stone #9)

Silent As A Stone (Heart of Stone #10)

Heart of Stone Volume Three

All of Me (Heart of Stone #11)

CLUB X SERIES

Temptation (Club X #1)

Surrender (Club X #2)

Possession (Club X #3)

Satisfaction (Club X #4)

Acceptance (Club X #5)

Complete Club X Series Box Set

NeXt SERIES

Notorious (NeXt #1)

Infamous (NeXt #2)

Ravenous (NeXt #3)

Ambitious (NeXt #4)

Flirtatious (NeXt #5)

Mysterious (NeXt #6)

Sensuous (NeXt #7)

Desirous (NeXt #8)

CORRUPTED LOVE TRILOGY

If I Dream (Corrupted Love #1)

If You Fight (Corrupted Love #2)

If We Fall (Corrupted Love #3)

Corrupted Love Trilogy Box Set

ADDICTED TO YOU SERIES

Crave (Addicted To You #1)

Adore (Addicted To You #2)

Shatter (Addicted To You #3)

Claim (Addicted To You #4)

Addicted To You Series Box Set

PROJECT ARTEMIS SERIES

In The Darkness (Project Artemis #1)

After The Storm (Project Artemis #2)

Behind The Scenes (Project Artemis #3)

Project Artemis Box Set

FINDING THE ONE SERIES

Hard Work (Finding The One #1)

Big Love (Finding The One #2)

DIRTY BOSS SERIES

Sweet Things (Dirty Boss #1)

Private Secretary (Dirty Boss #2)

Play Date (Dirty Boss #3)

Dirty Boss Volume One

K.M.'S BOOKS ARE IN AUDIOBOOK TOO!

BOOKS BY K.M. SCOTT WRITING AS GABRIELLE BISSET

SONS OF NAVARUS SERIES

Vampire Dreams Revamped (A Sons of Navarus Prequel)

Blood Avenged (Sons of Navarus #1)

Blood Betrayed (Sons of Navarus #2)

Longing (A Sons of Navarus Short Story)

Blood Spirit (Sons of Navarus #3)

The Deepest Cut (A Sons of Navarus Short Story)

Blood Prophecy (Sons of Navarus #4)

Blood Craving (Sons of Navarus #5)

Blood Eclipse (Sons of Navarus #6)

Blood Ascendant (Sons of Navarus #7)

The Sons of Navarus Box Set #1

The Sons of Navarus Box Set #2

DESTINED ONES DUET

Stolen Destiny (Destined Ones Duet #1)

Destiny Redeemed (Destined Ones Duet #2)

VICTORIAN EROTIC ROMANCES

Love's Master

Masquerade

The Victorian Erotic Romance Trilogy